BLUNTED ON REALITY

BLUNTED ON REALITY

A Young Man's View on Love, Career, and a President

by
Chinedu Achebe

Chinedu Books
Houston, Texas

BLUNTED ON REALITY

Published by:
Chinedu Books
9449 Briarforce Drive
Houston, TX 77063
wcachebe@hotmail.com

Chinedu Achebe, Publisher
Deborah Rene Jackson, Editor
Quality Press, Production Coordinator
Blackworks, Cover and Text Layout

© Copyright 2012 by Chinedu Achebe
ISBN #: 978-0-615-62925-4
Library of Congress Control #: 2012906922

DEDICATION

To E Joyce:

I would like to thank God for placing you in my life at the time that he did. Even though we have only known each for a short period of time, you have truly been a blessing to me as I have faced professional/ personal setbacks while finishing up this book. Your friendship, words of encouragement, and overall love and support has been very endearing to me. I know you are the woman I always envisioned that God had planned for me to be with. I pray that God will continue to bless you and me as we grow with each other toward forming a long term and permanent union together with him at the center of it. I love you, babe.

ACKNOWLEDGEMENTS

To my Mom & Dad:

I am forever grateful to God for giving me such loving parents. Whether in happy or trying times, you always showed unrelenting support for me. Even in the times that we didn't agree on things, you still offered a helping hand or advice for whatever I was doing. Thank you for instilling in me, Ijeoma, and Chukwuma the concept of hard work, putting your family first, and giving God the glory for everything we have in this world. I love you guys so much and I hope when the day comes that God gives me the opportunity for parenthood, that I can live up to the legacy you have left for me to follow.

CHAPTER ONE

Man I can't believe I got that wasted last night. Fuck it. We celebrated Obama's becoming the first black President of the United States.

Obi rose from his long night of partying and saw the flood of text messages. With all of the excitement around President Obama; Obi had almost forgotten about his own birthday. Today he turned 29-years-old and life had been pretty good for him, so far.

Obinna Ikechukwu Ifeanyi was born in Abagana, which is located in Anambra State, Nigeria. "Obi" grew up in Lagos, Nigeria where his father was an engineer at Shell and his mother was a professor at a private university. Obi is the oldest of three siblings; he has one sister and one brother. When Obi was only 8-years-old; the family moved to the U.S. after Obi's father was transferred by his job to Houston, Texas.

It didn't take Obi long to assimilate into the U.S. culture, particularly learning about black Americans. Education was focused on by Obi's parents, especially as Obi became a huge NBA fan and desired to play basketball. Although he acquired a desire to play basketball; Obi started placing more emphasis on his college plans and landed an academic scholarship to the University of Houston. Even though he planned on going to law school, Obi decided to double major in accounting and finance. After graduating from the University of Houston, Obi went to the only school he had always dreamed of going to: Howard Law School in Washington, D.C. It was at Howard that Obi developed his desire to do his part to help in the black community. The person he wanted to model himself after was Thurgood Marshall. Marshall was the first Black Supreme Court justice and attorney for the Brown versus Board of Education Supreme Court case ruling that separate but equal was unconstitutional in regards to education between white and black students.

Obi did a lot of pro bono legal work for low income residents who had issues with their landlords in the projects. After he graduated from law school, Obi got a job at his uncle's law firm; Ifeanyi and Associates back in Houston where he worked as a contract real estate and tax attorney. Obi sought new challenges, although this job paid well; he began to think about making an impact within the black community. Obi thought about the promise he made to his grandma before she died. That promise included helping his village of Abagana in Nigeria.

Obi remembers vividly his grandma telling his siblings, "Don't let the white man make you forget about your family in Nigeria. You came out of the ground in Igboland and that is where you come from. . We people back at home are counting on you guys to provide help for those of us who don't have." Obi sometimes wondered if he would ever get to do any of those things.

It seemed easy in his head in law school to be idealistic about changing the world, but in reality things are harder and more complicated to get done outside the walls of academia.

Obi was still pondering his future and gathering sleep when he received a call from his ex-girlfriend, Tamika Jones. "Happy birthday honey, how are you doing?" Tamika asked..

"Thanks, I am cool and just waking up."

"Well I am about to pull into your complex. Do you remember I said I would come over yesterday to see you?" Obi was puzzled and pretty much forgot what he said to her the previous day.

"Well that's cool I will meet you at my door in a few minutes," Obi said to Tamika. It seemed within seconds; Tamika was already at the door. She was carrying a bag full of groceries and Obi stared at how fine she looked in her tight jeans. He was getting hard just looking at her.

"So I was going to make you a birthday breakfast consisting of pancakes, eggs, and bacon," Tamika said. Obi responded, "That is cool with me. I am just going to jump in the shower real quick while you cook the food." In the shower, Obi reflected on his relationship with Tamika. He met her in his economics class during his sophomore year. Even though Tamika came off as bourgeoisie and pretentious, Obi was infatuated with her. Tamika was in Alpha Kappa Alpha Sorority, which had some of the finest black women on campus and they usually got jocked by athletes and other black fraternities.

Obi was pretty much a regular guy on campus, which was different from the type of guys Tamika dated. They usually consisted of guys with a thug appeal and classified as "playas". Obi was a calm, nice guy who just studied, went to a few parties, and played pickup basketball games at the gym. So it wasn't a shock when Tamika turned Obi down when he tried to holla at her. Tamika knew Obi was a good guy but she wasn't ready to settle down and give him the commitment he deserved. She would always say to him; "Obi, you will make a great boyfriend and potential husband to some woman one day. At this moment I am not the one for you right now. But if you are still single when I am looking, I will definitely talk to you."

Eventually as Tamika began to see Obi come into his own and his potential start to blossom, she knew she couldn't let a good guy like him pass her by. Also Tamika followed the trend of most women her age; after the guys with the bad boy image disappoint you; run to the nice guys for safety. Regardless of the reasoning or rationale, Obi was happy to get Tamika after almost a year of chasing her. Obi felt that entering his last couple years of college that he had his career planned out and the woman of his dreams by his side. Unfortunately, Obi and Tamika's three year relationship had a lot of ups and downs. As much as Obi had treated Tamika like a queen, Tamika still wanted a man with a roughneck image. She felt that a man needed to put his woman in check if she got out of line. Obi thought that Tamika clung to this fake stereotypical view of a black man that was portrayed in movies and rap music.

It seems the only thing that the both of them never argued about was sex. They had great chemistry together and enjoyed each other. But the sex wasn't enough and Tamika broke up with Obi right before he went to law school after three years of being together. The end of the relationship was very hard on Obi. He considered Tamika not only his lover, but a close friend. He shared all his dreams with her and thought she would be his wife and the mother of his children one day. Tamika wasn't sure if Obi was the only guy she really was interested in and wanted to test her options out. The both of them still communicated with each other while Obi was in D.C., but it wasn't until he moved back to Houston that they started hanging out with each other again. Since the both of them weren't in a relationship; they went back to having sex with each other. It was a comfort that the both of them enjoyed, but recently Obi was wanting more than sex from Tamika.

As he was getting out of the shower, there was a knock on the bathroom door. Once he opened the door, Tamika came in with her 5 foot 9 inch dark skin, thick body frame, long black hair, with her supple breasts and "phat" ass booty only wearing a bra and thong. "Well I haven't given you my own personal birthday shower yet." Tamika whispered seductively in Obi's ear. Obi started laughing. "I have already taken a shower but I'm game to have another one." So they proceeded to having mind-blowing sex for the next 45 minutes. Even though Obi did want more from Tamika, he couldn't resist still fucking her. Obi had self restraint in almost everything in his life, except when it came to Tamika. For all the achievements he had gained so far in his life, he still felt like that 19-year-old sophomore that he was when he first met her.

After they had finished their session, they headed to Obi's bedroom. "Obi, you be playing this quiet, nonchalant role as a front. If only people knew how much of a freak you are they would be surprised. I can't walk right after all the fucking and eating of my pussy you be doing to me." Tamika said. It seems the only time Tamika would see Obi's rough and aggressive side would be during sex. That is why she loved having sex with Obi. But for her, she wished this side of Obi was more prevalent in his non sexual behavior. Obi laughingly said to Tamika, "The problem is that you know you got some good pussy and you be giving me your best." Tamika responded, "That may be true but I ain't done with you yet." As Tamika leaned over towards Obi, she started kissing on him again and then sucking his dick. Obi was saying to her, "Damn, girl do you ever stop." She said, "I am giving you extra because of your birthday."

After Obi busted two more nuts, he said to Tamika, "I need to get some food in my body to regain the energy I have lost from fucking you." While they enjoyed a late breakfast, they began to discuss the history of Obama's election. Obi started the conversation saying, "I still can't believe this racist ass country elected a black man named Barack Hussein Obama to be the President. I guess Bush fucked this country up so much that Americans were ready for a dramatic change. Regardless of the matter, it is all good with me. Tamika, you wouldn't imagine the electricity that was at the spot we were watching the election results at yesterday. It was like everybody knew he was going to win, but when CNN reported that Barack Obama would be the President-elect on the screen; the crowd erupted in a euphoria that I have never seen in my life. I was embracing everybody at the place, including people I didn't know. I can't even lie to you; I got real emotional and shed a few tears. It was one of those moments that everybody will be able to tell their kids and grandkids about."

Tamika also indicated the feeling was the same at the place she was at with her friends. She posed a question to Obi, "So how does it feel to be 29 and one year closer to the big 30?" Obi responded, "I guess I am just embracing it. I think sometimes people get caught up in reaching a particular age as needing to have reached a certain level of accomplishments. I now see that in life everything comes with time. But it does make me more introspective that I am not getting younger and that I need to start prioritizing what is important for the rest of my life as well." Tamika responded, "So are you ready to settle down, get married, and start a family?" Obi said, "At this point of my life I know I am ready for the right woman to come into my life. I guess it depends on if that woman is ready for a man like me."

The comment was not intended for Tamika, but she took it like it was. "Well everybody isn't ready to settle down at the same time, we all got our own time." Tamika said. "That's cool, but I am not going to hang around while someone decides if I am a good enough man or not. If that person doesn't recognize what she has in front of her, then maybe I am not the guy for her." Obi responded.

Tamika started pondering a lot of thoughts in her mind. She really loved being around Obi and wanted to be with him one day, but even though she just turned 30-yearsold; she was just getting into her advertising career and wasn't sure if she wanted to make a sacrifice for any man, including Obi. The other thing is she couldn't imagine giving up Obi to another woman. It was funny how life turns out. In college she would never worry about competing for the affection and attention of a man. She held all the cards and decided who she wanted to date. But in the world outside of college, the odds of meeting a tall, smart, and conversational man like Obi were very slim.

Tamika's dating experiences after breaking up with Obi were not very successful. She didn't want the Obi type of guy, so she reverted back to the type of guys she dated before Obi. Even though in her early to mid 20s, the roughneck niggas were her thing, lately she finally realized that those weren't the type of guys to build a future with. The problem with Tamika was that she never fully appreciated Obi's scope of knowledge on political and social issues. She wasn't a very engaging conversational person beyond discussing the entertainment industry.

Tamika thought Obi's knowledge consisted of a wide variety of things like fluff which didn't amount to anything. She would always wonder why he liked to know what was going on in the world. Obi would be upset with Tamika's lack on intellectual curiosity. He would tell her, "I don't understand how you know almost everything about these damn reality shows, but you can't take 20 minutes to read the headline news from CNN on TV or the Internet." Tamika had never been asked to do much in her life but to smile and look beautiful. Most men never demanded her to challenge them mentally. But with Obi things were different. He was a very strong willed, outspoken, and opinionated man. He came from a family growing up where his father would have him read the New York Times by the time Obi was 10-years-old. Obi would have to write a thorough analysis of what he read. Both of his parents challenged their kids to be critical thinkers and not just memorize things or just regurgitate them.

Tamika and Obi grew silent for awhile as they watched TV. "Well Obi I know you are a good man and I hope we can someday make this thing work out between us; if not you will get yourself a great woman." Obi looked at Tamika with a sign of disappointment. Just when he thought she would make her appeal to really want to get back with him; she reverted back to grandstanding. In Obi's mind, this wasn't undergrad and his days of chasing and trying to make a woman want to be with him were over. He responded back to her, "I guess we will just see want happens."

After about another 30 minutes, Tamika started to get ready to head back home. As the both of them walked outside toward Tamika's car, they caught themselves holding each other's hands. "I really enjoyed you coming over, fixing breakfast, and the birthday shower," Obi said laughingly. Tamika said, "No problem. I don't mind doing anything for you. I know you, Chike, and Lamar are going to be in the streets tonight. Call me when you guys are done partying so you can come over to my place and we can pick up where we left off."

"Well I am going to have to take a quick nap to get ready for all of that," Obi responded.

They embraced and Tamika gave him a big kiss on the lips and started towards his ears. Once, Tamika pulled off; Obi went inside and fell asleep.

Later the phone rang and it was Obi's cousin, Chike Ifeanyi. "My president is African, my Toyota is blue, and I'll be Goddamn if my rims ain't too. What the fuck is going on man?" Chike yelled that into the phone after singing his own remixed lyrics from Young Jeezy's song, *'My President is Black'.* "Hey, Obi what have you been doing today? I know we had a long night yesterday, but I hope you are ready for your birthday celebration." Obi responded to him, "Well Chike, I have been good. I just had a long morning and you won't guess who stopped by my place." Chike responded, "Obi, I ain't into this guessing game shit. Who was it?"

Obi said, "Tamika, stopped by for a little bit. She cooked me some food and gave me some ass." Chike let out a gasp over the phone. "Obi, are you still fucking with her? Cousin, I thought you told me after the stunt she pulled on you before you went to law school that you were done with her. Obi you can't keep letting her jump in and out of your life. You turned 29 today and you have been dealing with Tamika for 10 years and what is she talking about. She is still the same girl from college that you were stuck on stupid for." Obi finally jumped in after Chike's long-winded tirade. "Dude, I didn't call her. She called me; saying she was on the way to my place. I never said I was going to get back with her, I was just explaining my story to you."

Chike said, "Obi, I have known you your whole life and you are a muthafuckin' liar. Your problem is that you are addicted to that pussy. Tamika has a mental and physical strangle hold on your mind and dick that you can't and don't want to shake loose."

Obi started to get annoyed with the conversation and decided to change the topic. "Anyway, Chike, I am thinking about going to D.C. for this inauguration in January. Are you trying to go?" Chike said, "Hell yeah; if my funds are okay. I will definitely fool with it. You talk with Lamar about hitting it up." "I will bring it up too when we hang out tonight at the Chill Spot," Obi said. "That's a bet Obi, so what time are you trying to hit it up?" Obi responded to Chike's question, "Let's shoot for between 8 to 9 p.m. to catch the end of the late night happy hour and then hit up a club." Chike agreed and he said he would call Lamar and inform him of the plans for the evening.

As he hung up the phone with Chike, Obi thought about the conversation about Tamika. He knew Chike had a point and was just looking out for him. Chike was three years older than Obi and even though they were cousins, they had more of a big brother and little brother relationship. Ever since he moved to the states, Chike always looked out for him from beef with dudes to dating issues with the females. But the only problem with Chike is that he sometimes wanted you to take his advice all the way through without any objections.

As Obi turned on the television, all the channels were talking about the historic election victory for Barack Obama. He began to recollect how he had first thought Hillary Clinton would win the primaries and how Barack didn't seem like he was ready to take the mantle from her. Obi had always been a fan of Barack dating back to his 2004 speech during the Democratic National Convention. He felt that Obama might be able to bring a new level of excitement and energy to politics that the Bush years had sapped from the country. But he wasn't sure if a black man could be president and if Obama would be able to contend with Hillary Clinton along with her husband, former president Bill Clinton. Well, to everyone's surprise he won a tough primary against her and then cruised forward to beat John McCain in the general election.

Obi wondered if Obama could take his uplifting campaign rhetoric and actually form policies that would help the country come out of the terrible recession. He also wanted to see if the economic problems, which have hampered black people in America for hundreds of years, would actually be addressed by this president. But today wasn't the time to discuss the future; hell Obama wouldn't technically be the president until January 20th 2009. Obama's election also made Obi think about himself as well. Even though he was progressing in his own career, he was looking for his signature moment that would define him. It seems like Obama generated a lot of attention for other things beyond politics.

On many African American blogs and magazines, they were trying to depict Barack and Michelle Obama, and their family as the real life Huxtables. The Huxtables were the family portrayed on The Cosby Show. It seems everyone became enamored by the idea of the Obamas reshaping the shattered relationship between the black man and black woman, as well as making it cool to be smart and black. But to Obi, Barack and Michelle represented something deeper than the superficial stuff people wanted them to be. In his book, 'Dreams of My Father', Barack discussed how he first met his wife at the law firm he was interning at while he was in law school.

He talked about how he drove a raggedy car, had shoes with holes in them and styled badly worn out clothes.

President Obama's soon to be wife had finished law school and was already an associate at the firm. Obi admired Barack for winning over Michelle not with any game, but just by being himself. He also liked how Michelle was able to see beyond the surface and see a man who had potential to do great things. It was interesting to see that on their first date, they went to the park and saw the Spike Lee movie, 'Do the Right Thing'. It seems laughable today that a black woman of Michelle's status would ever give a guy like Barack a chance. It was funny to hear women talk about how they wanted to find their own Barack, but most of them only thought that having a college degree with a job made them a good enough woman to be married. Unfortunately, since leaving law school, Obi rarely met those eclectic black women who were intellectually and culturally provocative and thought outside of the box.

As of late, he was just meeting women who weren't very conversational about anything and considered traveling to different places their hobby. But he also started to realize that at 29, the window was closing on finding the woman truly desirable and now the focus was to find a woman with some level of compatibility. Still pondering his dating dilemma, Obi took a look at his cell phone and saw that his mom had left him a voicemail wishing him a happy birthday.

He called his mother back, "Hi, mama how are you doing?" "Obi, I am fine. Happy birthday my son; how is your day going?" Obi responded, "It was going well mama. I am recuperating from all of the excitement last night. I can't believe Obama will be the president." Obi's mom agreed and said, "Yes it is good to see a son of Africa climb to the highest office in this country. As I always tell you guys,

Chineke (God) had already destined for him to be president. I only hope that he will continue to protect him and his family from those who wish harm against him. Obi's mom turned the conversation back on him. "So my son, when are you going to settle down and get married? You are now 29-years-old and you can't continue to live this playboy lifestyle with Chike. Your father has some friends in the Nigeria Club with eligible daughters to set you up with. Just let us know so we can start the process." Obi grudgingly said, "Mama, we will talk about this matter when I come home this weekend. I was just calling you back from earlier. I have to go get ready for the evening. I love you and I will talk to you later."

With disgust in her voice, his mother said, "Okay, well be careful wherever you go tonight." Obi loved his mom for wanting to help him out, but unfortunately, she didn't think physical appearance in picking a woman was important. She was more concerned about what career the person selected and if they were a nice person. He usually relied on his sister, Chinwe, to check on the women to see if they fit his standards.

Obi got a text message from Chike telling him that Lamar and he were on the way to the Chill Spot. Obi started to get dressed and make his way out towards his destination. While driving, he started to think about the great times with his friends at The Chill Spot. Even though it was a regular soul food restaurant, the place would be jumping on the weekends. Obi and his friends started going there during his sophomore year of college and continued up till today. . Even when Obi would come home from law school, he would make it a point to go to the Chill Spot. Beyond the great food and strong margaritas, it was a great place to see women after the club and also have freewheeling conversations ranging from women to sports.

Obi started to reflect on the countless numbers he got from going there along with the many females he messed with because of it. The Chill Spot was always the gift that kept on giving. By the time he had realized it, Obi had pulled up at The Chill Spot. As he got out of the car, he headed toward the patio and saw Lamar and Chike.

"There he goes; the birthday boy is in the house. I thought you were done after all that drinking you did last night. You know if you didn't come through I would have called you out," Lamar said. "I know you would have, nigga. All you do is live to talk shit," Obi said. Lamar Smith is Obi's best friend from college. They both met in freshman orientation playing pickup basketball and have been cool ever since. If Chike was considered to be Obi's older brother, Lamar was Obi's alter ego. Lamar took more chances in life and had more game when it came to women. Even though Obi was very smart and played basketball in high school; he was relatively quiet and shy when it came to talking to girls. He usually got girls from one of his teammates putting him down and the girl just being taken away with him because he played basketball. Even though he got his share of girls; he never got the ones he really wanted. He also knew that going to college would be different and the girls wouldn't know him. He would actually have to talk to them. Lamar taught him to use his height to his advantage and he would say, "Obi, nigga, you 6 foot 4 inches and these chicks will be on your dick."

Lamar would also tell him that he should treat women the same regardless of how fine or ugly they are. Lamar's favorite quote was short and simple. He would say, "Treat the rocks and stars the same. The problem with niggas is that they be giving these fine ass chicks preferential treatment. I tell all these hoes the only thing I can give 'dem is a hard dick and bubble gum." Obi had come a long way from those early days, but Lamar still chimed in when needed.

"So I hear you went back to fucking Tamika again, Obi." Obi glanced at Chike and then back at Lamar to answer the question.

Lamar started chuckling, "Obi you know that Chike can't hold water. So what's 'da deal?" Obi began telling Lamar about everything that went down with him and Tamika from earlier in the day. Obi liked having both Chike and Lamar around for these types of discussions. He knew that Chike would usually give him a more measured approach while Lamar was more of a live for the moment type of person, which was good and bad depending on the situation. So Lamar asked Obi one question, "So what did Chike advise you to do? I know that nigga already gave his two cents about the matter." Chike jumped in to say, "Lamar, how do you know I told Obi anything?" Lamar started to laugh, "I know the both of you niggas like the back of my hand. Chike you always make your opinions known, so why wouldn't you on this matter?" Chike knew Lamar was right and began to laugh at the whole thing. So Obi continued and he said, "Chike told him to stop messing with Tamika."

Lamar started shaking his head and laughing, "Classic Chike, you always want to talk a nigga out of getting some pussy." Obi jumped to Chike's defense and said, "He might be right this time Lamar. I'm looking for more than just fucking from Tamika. I'm 29 and looking for a relationship." Lamar took a deep breath and said, "Obi, you are my boy, but I gotta be 100 percent honest with you. We both have known Tamika since college and real talk; she has always been full of shit. I know you love her and in a relationship with her, but you gotta change the way you deal with her. If she just wants you to beat up the pussy, that ain't a bad thing. In the meanwhile you are getting some Grade A pussy at your disposal while you find the right woman.

20

If Tamika finally grows up and learns she needs to stop chasing these worthless ass niggas and wants to fuck with you strong, then she can make that decision for herself." Both Chike and Obi started laughing uncontrollable for five minutes after Lamar finished talking. Obi said to Lamar, "My nigga you are probably one of the most off da chain muthafuckas I know." Lamar said to the both of them, "I'm just trying to put ya'll on some game. You know I stay knee deep in pussy while ya'll have desert dick and go home to jack off to some pornos on TV."

Obi said jokingly, "Well, Lamar thanks for your great words of wisdom. But anyway I told Chike that I am trying to go to D.C. for this inauguration during January. I was going to ask you if you are interested in going up there." Lamar responded, "I will have to check my finances, work schedule, and I will get back with you. There will be a lot of eligible black women out there. It will be like the Essence Festival times 10 up there. You should definitely try and go if you can." Obi responded, "I know there will be tons of women and parties going on, but for me it is really about being part of history. I hope this can start the foundation for black people trying to come together." Lamar said to Obi sarcastically, "Well you can be soul brotha during the day and holla at females at night." Obi didn't take kindly to the reference made by Lamar and told him, "Is everything with you about just fucking with women? What else do you want for yourself?"

Lamar said to Obi, "Well, look man everybody ain't on this black empowerment trip like you are on. If you wanna be Malcolm X Jr., then be my guest. But you better worry about improving yourself and stop worrying about trying to save the black race. Shit, we got a black president; what else do you want?" Obi said to Lamar, "We as black people have to strive for more than just wanting to be rappers and athletes. We have to understand our past, our present, and try to change our future. I hope that Obama's election isn't just some watershed moment in the nation's history, but hopefully it will begin a change in the mentality of black people." Chike finally came and said, "Ya'll boys calm that shit down. Tonight is the night for celebration, not arguing." Chike wasn't in the mood for da bullshit and didn't feel like taking sides on the discussion, but he agreed with Lamar.

He didn't have this desire to deal with black American issues because he was Nigerian. He thought things needed to be done, but felt the problems were for actual black Americans with roots in this country. He nevertheless loved Obi's passion about the matter and his willingness to be a part of the changes going on. Chike saw the positive effect going to Howard had on Obi and how it had changed him. Chike knew since they were kids that Obi was a conversationalist. He always wanted to have discussions with everyone. Chike's father picked up on that early in Obi's life and told him that he will be a lawyer one day like himself. Chike never told Obi about how he was very proud of him growing into the man he is today.

As the three of them started to think about places to go, Obi began to think about the conversation that he and Lamar were just having. Unfortunately, Lamar represented the type of black person that Obi was talking about. When Lamar was in college, he had a lot of ambition. He had majored in finance and wanted to be financial advisor. Even though he got his degree, Lamar became stagnant about his life. He bounced around from different jobs and currently was a manager at a retail store. Some people had a vice for drugs or alcohol, but for Lamar it was pussy. Before going to law school, the both of them talked about possibly starting a small business. But it seems like their friendship wasn't as strong as it once was.

Lamar never came up to visit Obi in D.C. and they rarely talked on the phone. It seemed like Lamar's carefree lifestyle had taken over what his priorities were.

Chike finally blurted out to Lamar and Obi, "I heard Club H is supposed to be jumping tonight; you guys wanna fool with it?" Obi was reluctant to go another hard night of partying and wanted to do something more low key. He convinced Chike and Lamar to go to Boca Lounge and they decided to head up there to beat the crowd. On most nights Boca usually was pretty chill. But with Obama winning the election the night before; the parking lot was jam-packed. It seemed like every black person in Houston wanted to come out and show their love for Obama.

As they got out of their cars and walked toward the line of the lounge; the excitement from the night before was still in the air. The three of them were approached by a random dude who told them, "My niggas these white folks can't tell us nothing tonight. My president is muthafuckin black and you know they hate that shit." As the dude continued to walk by he gave Obi, Lamar, Chike and damn near everybody in line a fist bump. Lamar said, "That dude is drunk as hell, but he is just enjoying the moment. I know I can't say that I'm mad at him. For all the bullshit black people go through on a daily basis; we deserve a few days of excitement for this achievement." Obi felt the same way about the matter.

Even though 99 percent of black people didn't know Obama, they all felt like he was collectively their distant cousin who had made the family proud. He was the embodiment of older black Americans who had to defer their dreams because of racial discrimination. He also provided hope to the younger generation that all things were possible, even a black man being president of the United States.

After a half hour of waiting in the line, the three of them finally got into the spot. Lamar came out and threw the gauntlet down, "I know y'all boys saw all type of ass coming in here. So I wanna know who is down to fuck with these women tonight." Chike started laughing and said, "This nigga Lamar never gets tired of being on da hoes." Lamar said back to him, "I live by the words of Notorious B.I.G.; "Money, hoes, and clothes all a nigga knows.""

The three of them usually went out to see who could get the most numbers by the end of the night. It was done for ego purposes and to add to each dude's respective roster. Obi used to relish getting numbers, but recently he was getting nowhere with meeting women at the clubs or bars. Most of the time, the numbers game, resulted in either the women not answering the phone or not having any compatibility with him. As the three of them split up, Obi started to approach the bar to get a drink. On the way there, he caught eyes with a nice brown skin female. Obi reached out his arm and grabbed her hand to get her attention. He asked, "So what is your name?" She responded, "Aisha."

Obi proceeded to tell her his name. Aisha said, "So you are Nigerian right?" Obi responded jokingly, "Yeah, I'm Nigerian. Is there a problem with that?" She said, "I don't fuck with Nigerians; I just talk to regular American black men." As he began to look at Aisha with a dazed look he said to her, "Nigerians are black, the only thing is our ethnicity is different from black people born in the U.S." Then Aisha bluntly said, "Look I dated a Nigerian man before and he was overly aggressive and wanted me to go along with his tribal-and cultural bullshit, if we got married."

Obi shook his head in disbelief and decided to throw one more question at her. "So who did you vote for in the elections?"

She shouted out with glee, "Barack." Obi said, "So you do realize his father was Kenyan and his full name is Barack Hussein Obama." She said, "Well I'll vote for an African I just won't date one." When he saw the conversation with her was going nowhere, Obi picked up his drink and told Aisha to have a good evening.

In his head he thought, "This stupid bitch, what the fuck is she talking about." Obi didn't let the bullshit from Aisha fuck up his night. He still was able to pull three numbers before the lounge closed down for the night. As he was heading toward the exit of Boca, he ran back into Lamar and Chike. "Obi, how many numbers did you get?" Lamar asked. Obi told him that he got three numbers. Lamar said, "That's not bad; there was plenty to choose from in here. Me and Chike got at two homegirls and we are about to grab some food with them." Obi asked how do they look and both Lamar and Chike tried their best to act like they didn't hear the question. Lamar finally said, "They "awright", both of them got some "phat" ass booties. Shit it doesn't matter anyway as long as they are face down ass up while I am fucking them." Both Lamar and Chike just shook their heads and started laughing uncontrollably. Chike asked Obi what he was about to do and he said that Tamika texted him to come over to her place. Lamar reminded Obi about their conversation at The Chill Spot earlier in the evening. Obi agreed and dabbed up both Chike and Lamar, then headed to his car.

Obi drove about 15 minutes to get to Tamika's house. He called her when he pulled into her parking lot. He walked toward her place and then knocked on the door. Tamika opened the door with only a bra and thong on again. "Man, I hope you don't greet everybody who comes to your place like that." Obi said. Tamika responded with a laugh, "No, this is only for you. Well I am happy you came so we can continue where we left off from this afternoon." Obi entered and the both of them headed toward the bedroom to have sex again.

CHAPTER TWO

A couple of days had passed since Obama's election night victory and Obi's birthday celebration. The excitement was great but it was time for things to get back to normal and that meant; it was time for Obi to head back to work. Along with being a lawyer, Obi was a CPA, which kept him busy around tax time and sometimes beyond that. But before the weekend would be over, he was going to his parents' house for a birthday gathering. He started to get dressed and was waiting for Chike to pick him up. While he was getting himself together, his younger sister, Chinwe, called him. She said, "Obinna, where are you? Mama and papa along with Uncle Ugochukwu and Auntie Nkiru are waiting on you and Chike." "We should be there in about 30 to 45 minutes. I am waiting for Chike to come. You know that guy can be very slow now."

"Both of you guys always drag your feet to go anywhere."

"I hear you. Anyway, how is school going for you right now?"

Chinwe was working on her Master's in Education at Texas Southern University. She is also a high school math teacher, but had plans to start a nonprofit educational foundation to help minority at risk kids. She said, "It's going great, after this fall semester I will be graduating in the spring." Obi said, "That's good, I am happy for you." Chinwe begrudgingly said, "Yeah, thanks. I just wish mom and dad were as enthusiastic about it. They are still upset that I didn't go to pharmacy school after I got my bachelors." Obi told her, "Chinwe, you are now 26-years-old. You have to do what is best for you, and not what our parents think you should do. Well anyway, I have to finish getting ready before Chike comes over. So let us finish this conversation later. " Chinwe said, "Okay, that's cool. I will see you guys in a little while."

As he hung up the phone with his sister; Obi could relate to what his sister was going through with his parents. Obi's parents subscribed to the same ideology that most Nigerian parents did, which was to predetermine their child's career at an early age and steer them into doing that. Their kids were relegated to three fields in this order: medical, engineering, and business. In Obi's case he was supposed to be an engineer. He was good at math and didn't think of why he wouldn't major in that field when he got to college. But by his sophomore year at U of H; things started to change for him. He was struggling in his engineering classes and didn't feel obligated or motivated to stay in that major any more. At the end of that semester, he changed his major to finance and accounting. His parents were disappointed with the decision; they felt Obi had given up and wasn't trying hard enough. Eventually his mother accepted that Obi had to do what he wanted, but his father, who was an engineer, still resisted Obi on his decision.

This disagreement pretty much damaged their relationship. The both of them rarely spoke to each other on the phone or when Obi stopped by the house. Even after he finished from undergrad and went to law school; nothing really changed regarding the father and son relationship. Obi wished things were different, but felt he had to live his own life regardless of what his father or anybody else thought. There were times that Obi felt that his father was not worried about Obi's happiness, but more concerned about status and rank among the Nigerians in Houston. Obi's father was the Honorable Chief Engineer Chukwuemeka Ifeanyi; he was president of the social group; The Nigerian Club. He was also a part of other Igbo related organizations in the city as well as in Nigeria. Obi was a testament of the competitiveness that Nigerians had about the achievement of their kids, but felt it was driving many of their kids to please their parents instead of themselves.

Obi heard a knock at his door and it was Chike. "Damn, nigga you are later than a muthafucka," Obi said jokingly.

Chike replied, "Man you always are late to shit as well."

They both laughed at each other at the acknowledgement of their consistent and mutual lateness. The two men took Obi's car to his parents' house. On the way a conversation between both guys started. Chike asked Obi, "So how do think Boca Lounge was the night of your birthday? You said you got three phone numbers so it looks like you did well."

Obi responded, "To be honest, cousin, I probably won't even call those chicks. It was just some sport fishing. I didn't have any real interest in those women. Real deal, Chike, I am getting tired of dealing with these black American woman. It feels like it doesn't matter what environment you are in; they are always on some bullshit.

I tried going up to a couple of women to start a conversation about the whole Obama thing, but they just looked at me like I had shit on my face. It seems like these women keep screwed up faces on at all times, even when you try and talk with them respectfully."

Chike started shaking his head and said to Obi, "I feel you cousin. That is why I don't mess too much with these black American women. They can't respect a dude that talks to them with sense. If you talk the way Lamar be talking to them, they stay on your dick. If you try and treat them with a small form of respect, they call you a nice guy or a square ass nigga. Neither of us was raised to treat women harshly, so I know it is not in your character to do so."

Obi said, "It sometimes feels like with black people that even though we are grown up; we still have this high school mentality to dating. We still want to judge everyone by how fly you dress, how much swag you got, and who can be the best playa. It feels like every time we go to a black spot I can turn back the clock to 1998. It is sad to say, but we are mostly about style with little to no substance."

Chike told Obi, "I couldn't have said it better myself. I always say that black women won't date average black men. I be hearing these chicks say they want a corporate thug. They say it is a guy who can work a regular 9 to5 and also have some hood in him as well. That to me is the biggest bunch of bullshit I have heard in my life. Do you think white, Hispanic, Asian, or African women ask for this with who they date? No, they do not. It is always funny that black American women ask for all types of shit in the world out of black men, but 42 to45 percent of these women over 25 years old aren't married. I am not trying to say that it is all their faults, because there are a lot of terrible niggas for them to choose from. But at least give a decent dude a chance to see what he is talking about."

Chike continued to say, "I will just stay with my Nigerian women. I know some of them be on some different shit, but for most of them we know how they were raised and can somewhat deal with their stuff. But I will tell you one thing that will change my mind and that is Obama's inauguration in January. If you go there you will get all different spectrums of black women. All these types of women are looking for the young professional dudes like you. These women will be the type of women who you need right now. But the key is most of these women are in their late 20s to early 30s. They already know what they want in a man and they are secure as well. It's not like fucking with these stupid chicks in their early to mid 20s; still chasing some dude who will buy them a drink at a club or are impressed by someone taking them to eat at an expensive restaurant. Man, real talk you need to start making your arrangements to get out there right away. You know the price of tickets will be going up fast."

Obi agreed with everything that Chike said. He asked him if he would go and Chike said, "Cousin, I don't think I am going to be able to make it. I got money committed to other things. This might be a solo mission for you. But heck you went to law school out there so I know you got some classmates who are either still up there or will be going out there for it." Obi asked Chike if Lamar told him anything about going and he responded, "Obi, I know that is your boy. But he ain't talking about shit. I hate to say this but this ain't the event for him. You gotta actually have some real conversations with these women, not the bullshit parking lot pimping he be doing. I love hanging out with that dude, but he gotta grow up. Both of ya'll damn near 30 years old and he still be trying to fuck everything that moves. I will tell you like I tell him repeatedly; this dating shit gets harder the older you become. The odds of getting a woman with no kids and no issues, decreases for all of us dudes every day. My advice to you is to take advantage of this opportunity, take your ass to D.C. and try to find your Mrs. Ifeanyi."

Obi started laughing and said to Chike, "You are a fool cousin, but I agree with your assessment." Chike asked Obi, "So now that your birthday has passed what are your goals for 29 and beyond?" Obi responded, "You know what cousin, I'm still figuring that out. Beyond settling down with the right woman, I feel like wanting to do more with my life. Maybe doing more to help black community groups with legal and economic matters." Chike looked at Obi and said, "I know that my father put this whole pro black-African streak in you and you still seem committed to trying to improve the lives of others."

Chike's path wasn't as clear though. Even though he was 32-years-old, he didn't have any real plans. Chike graduated from college and got his degree in management and was a claims adjuster for an insurance company. His father wanted him to do more with his career, but Chike became complacent in what he was doing and never really tried to do anything else. Chike was a happy go lucky guy who just lived life day to day. The logic he used was great when you are in your early 20s, but as you begin to approach your mid 30s, you are expected to have some type of outline of how you want your life to go.

Chike was the youngest of the three kids between his mom and dad. His older brother, Chidi, was a pharmacist and his older sister, Ngozi, was a nurse. Chike's father had wanted him to go into law so he could possibly take over his law firm when he retired. But when Chike didn't seem that interested in law school, Chike's father started directing his attention to his nephew, Obi. "You know my pops keeps telling me to go back to school and get my MBA and move into management at my company. I don't think my father understands that everybody ain't into going to school." Chike said.

Obi told him, "I feel that but it can't hurt you to get it, regardless if you stay where you are at or move into another company or industry." Chike responded, "I will think about it and make a decision." By the time they knew it they had arrived at Obi's parents' house. Obi's mother had greeted them as they entered the house.

"How are you two guys doing? We have been waiting on your arrival." Obi said, "Mama, I am sorry for our lateness, you know how Chike is always running late."

Chike jumped in and said laughingly, "Auntie, don't believe him. You know your son is very slow at dressing himself." Obi's mother began to laugh and said to them, "You two have been arguing since you were small boys. Now go to the kitchen, wash your hands, and get ready to eat."

As they both walked towards the kitchen, the smell of jelof rice and plantation had permeated throughout the house. Once they got into the kitchen they saw that Obi's father along with Chike's father and mother were already eating their food. Chike's father shouted out to them, "So how are you two playboys doing?" Chike answered him back, "We are doing well father, just trying to bring the birthday boy here to have his celebration." Chike's mother asked, "So, Obi how does it feel to be 29? You have one more year until the big 30."

Obi responded, "Well Auntie, I feel great. You just have to thank Chineke for all his blessings and hope for continued health to accomplish one's goals." Everyone in the room shook their heads in agreement with his statement.

Obi's father jokingly interjected by saying, "Well said my son.

Now it's time for you to find yourself a good woman to settle down with and get married." Obi told him, "Papa, finding a woman is easy. Getting one that is the right fit for me is difficult." Obi's father looked in awe in hearing the comment from his son. "Obi and Chike, you youngsters make this dating thing too complicated. The problem is that in this country you have many options without any guidance. During me and Ugo's time, your family helped with making decisions. For example, if we saw a girl we were interested in; the first person to do some behind the scene investigation would be our sister. Our sister would speak to other girls and find out about the reputation of the girl and also determine if personalities would match up. As you guys know, we men are too focused on physical attributes at times and that can blind us from noticing that the girl might be a tough person for us to handle."

Obi's father continued to say, "If everything came up fine, the next step would be for one to learn what type of family the girl comes from. That usually involved asking neighbors or people from around the way. If that is a go, then the boy and girl would date and see how things worked out. If our parents had friends with girls of dating age; they would encourage us to talk with the girl and see if there was any common interest. Neither of those scenarios I presented involved any sort of forcing someone on the person or any meddling into anything. I feel that too many divorces happen in this country because everyone wants to make all the decisions themselves. People just jump into marriage like nothing and sometimes without the consultation of any family or even close family friends. So I hope you guys have gotten the drift of my conversation."

Obi and Chike knew this long-winded talk by Obi's father was just not for him to hear himself talk. It pretty much meant to say that you guys have had your way in dating to no avail and now we think you should consider our way. By this time Obi's mother had come to the kitchen and jumped right into the conversation. "Obi, we know that you had a difficult time dealing with the breakup of Tamika a few years back. I know since you have been in law school until now I haven't heard you talk about anyone seriously. But maybe it is time to pull your eyes from dating these akata girls." Obi's mother never said anything about him dating Tamika or thought she was a bad person, but just preferred that her kids date Nigerians. If not a Nigerian, she wouldn't mind someone from another African country or the Caribbean.

Obi's parents didn't dislike akatas (black Americans), but felt that their lack of culture would influence their own kids to not follow theirs if they got married. They also heard stories from other Nigerians about black American women refusing to take their husband's Nigerian name, not wanting their kids to have Nigerian names, or go to Nigeria and see their relatives. The final thing was the akata women refusing to learn to cook Nigerian foods. Chike's mother also felt the same way as her sister-in-law and put her two cents into the discussion. "Madam, you are right. These akata women want these rough guys who beat on them. Obi and Chike you boys are too quiet for them. They will run circles around you guys and your lives will be very terrible. Abeg now. Listen to your mothers before it gets too late."

Both Ugo and Chukwuemeka began to stare at each other in amazement as they heard their wives go on about this topic. Ugo decided to jump in and try and stop the conversation, "Nkiru and Ijeoma let's cool down the argument. These boys have heard your plea and will keep it in mind." Both men had different views on the subject of dating. Obi's father agreed with his wife, but didn't want to come out as bold as his wife did. Chike's father preferred that he marry a Nigerian woman, but he knew that a lot of Nigerian women weren't easy to deal with as well and didn't want to put them on a pedestal as the best choice. He had two black American women in his law office and felt that his wife and sister-in-law were making wild generalizations that weren't true. But he also wasn't in the mood for a long drawn argument with his wife and decided to take the diplomatic route.

Ugo decided to move the conversation toward the election of Obama. "So Obi and Chike, what do you think about this Obama victory a few nights ago? You young guys really went to the polls heavy for him." Obi responded by saying, "Well, Uncle, it was very exhilarating. I think everyone felt like they were taking part in a very historical moment in world history. But beyond the surface, I am interested to see if he puts Hillary Clinton in his cabinet and if so, what position he will give her. I would like to see who his economic advisers will be and gain some insight on what policies his administration will attack in his first 100 days."

Chike didn't have much to add but just to agree with Obi's point. Chike followed politics, but didn't get into the nuts and bolts like Obi did. Ugo enjoyed having these discussions with his nephew. He was usually very knowledgeable about what he was talking about and never said things out of emotion. Their talks went back to when Obi was in middle school. Even though Obi usually held his own at an early age; Ugo always gave him critiques to keep him from getting to cocky or arrogant. Ugo said, "Yeah, I think people will carefully be watching who he picks because by all estimates, the recession will be getting worse and he needs to pick guys who will bring some stability to the stock market. I will give him about one year before people start asking for his head. Americans have short memories and will forget that the foolish man named Bush caused most of the misery we are facing and will continue to endure for years to come."

Sometimes Ugo and Obi would get caught up in their own world and they would forget other people were in the room. Obi's father came in with his own analysis. "I don't think Obama can do too much to fix the economy in the next two years. His problem is that he has promised so much that people will have very high expectations, which I am not sure he can meet. People will expect him to be like Jesus Christ and turn water into wine. But regardless of the situation; to see an African man leading this country still makes me have great joy. Many of us like me and Ugo came to America for college in the late 60s and early 70s and can relate to Obama's father's trek."

"I have to state something though, that has been bothering me for awhile and it is how the news media has made Obama the savior for the black Americans. I expect that from whites, but what shocked me was your black news media. It seemed like they interviewed black civil rights leaders and others about his impact on the black American community. But did they talk with any Africans and ask us what we felt about him? The answer is no. Before he came into the U.S Senate, I read that black Americans in Chicago were saying that he wasn't black enough. But now that he has risen up to the top, you see how akatas are all trying to get a piece of him. They forget that he has African blood running in his veins. In my opinion, black Americans just like the symbol that Obama portrays. Most of them don't care much for us Africans, only when it is beneficial to them. When the white man is giving them hell, they run to us and call us their African brothers and sisters and say how we have to come together. But as soon as the white man treats them a little bit better, then they reject being called African and start referring to themselves as black. This is the game akatas have been playing for over 30 years with Africans in this country," said Obi's father.

As the rest his family was discussing the matter, Obi began to think about, the relationship between Africans and black Americans. On election night, the scene of joy on the television showing black people from Harlem, New York to Nairobi, Kenya was overwhelming. It seemed that for a brief period of time, Obama had united the black race as no one person or incident had done before. But it was also incorrect to believe that the divisions that separated these distant relatives could be fixed very easily. Each group had their own separate grievances, which weren't interrelated.

One thing that Obama did was to certify the excellence of Africans as ambitious and intellectual people. Even though Obama's scholastic achievement in college and law school was rare to black Americans; in the eyes of Africans, including Obi, this was the fabric of what was instilled in them by demanding parents who wouldn't settle for anything less than being the best.

As the conversation amongst his family continued, Uncle Ugo made his comments be known. "I would like to see Obama do more to engage in real dialogue with Africa. He could challenge African leaders and presidents to push for reforms to help their people have a more economic and social well-being. I think these useless leaders can't use any more excuses when they see their African brothers across the phone or table from them asking them to change their ways." Ugo was pretty much describing Nigeria in a nutshell. The country has the largest population on the continent of Africa and is among the top oil producing countries in the world.

To the dismay of many Nigerian citizens in the country and abroad, the government has used the oil revenue as their own personal slush fund to the tune of billions of dollars taken out of Nigeria's treasury that rendered the country useless. Many Nigerians wondered if gaining independence from Britain in 1960 and the discovery of oil was either a gift or a curse. A couple of years after the country gained its independence, there was severe tension and violence between the southeastern part of Nigeria, which consisted of the Igbo tribe, and the northern part of Nigeria, which was mainly Hausa. This correlated with the Igbos succeeding from Nigeria and naming their region, Biafra. This led to a brutal civil war between Nigeria and Biafra, which lasted from 1967 to 1970, and millions of people killed.

Eventually, the Biafrans conceded and the country was made whole again. But for many Igbos of Chike and Obi's parent's generation, the scars of the war had never left them. This began a string of military rule, which would besiege the country for the next 30 years. All of this left many people in the country seeing little hope for upward mobility. It caused a great number of talented Nigerians to make a mass exodus to Europe, the United States, and other countries.

Obi's mother responded to Ugo's assertion. "I don't think anybody can fix Nigeria. It is a very hopeless country." Ugo told her, "Ijeoma, have we not seen a miracle in a black man being president in this country. We all know the racial problems that this country faced and continues to face. Maybe I am an optimist, but I am not giving up on my country. We have been independent for less than 50 years and had a lot of instability in government. In the first 50 years of

American independence; they didn't fare that well either. I'm not sure if things will change in my lifetime, Chike's, or even my grandkids, but I think that Chineke will one day show his favor on our country and people." Aunt Nkiru jumped in and said, "I agree with my husband. Sometimes we are too critical of our country. Those back home are still living and breathing as we here are writing Nigeria's obituary. They have to do what they have to do make things happen. I admire the strength of our people to persevere regardless of what obstacles come their way."

While everyone was still talking, Obi's younger brother Okechukwu, nicknamed Okey, had come home. He was currently a junior at Texas A&M University and was majoring in electrical engineering. He came back from school for the weekend and to see his older brother. He walked toward the kitchen and was greeted by everyone. He told Obi happy birthday and hugged his parents, aunt and uncle. Okey tried to be funny and leave the room without saying anything to Chike. Chike said to Okey, "So now you are the big man on campus and can't greet me." Okey laughingly responded to Chike, "I purposely didn't say anything to get a reaction from you."

Okechukwu was the favorite of his dad because he was the youngest and usually did as he was told by his father. He majored in engineering even though he wasn't that into it. Obi would advise him to be more assertive in dealing with their father, but Okechukwu didn't like confrontation and usually just remained neutral on most matters regarding his parents.

Okechukwu was 23-years-old and Obi figured that he would eventually grow up and stop trying to please their father. Chike, Obi, and Okechukwu left the kitchen and headed to the living room to talk. "So how are the females treating you in College Station?" Chike asked. Okechukwu responded, "Its going okay cousin. There ain't too many black women up there." "So I guess you have to deal with what you got. I have fucked with a couple white and Hispanic girls, but I need the women with big booties and most of them don't have any. A couple chicks that I talk to; go to Prairie View A&M, so it's all good." Obi responded to him, "I see you young playa. I see that talks by Chike and me have helped you out with the females." Okechukwu laughed at him, "That choir boy shit ya'll was talking about was getting me no pussy. I had a few talks with Lamar and the pussy has been rolling in every since." Obi laughed and said, "That nigga Lamar does have a way with words for dealing with women."

As the three of them continued to talk, Obi's sister, Chinwe came into the living room. "So how are my three brothers doing?" Chinwe said. Chike responded, "We are all doing great my sister. So I see that my folks and your folks were hinting like they wanted to get into the match making game for me and Obi." Chinwe started to laugh and said to Chike, "Why should you be surprised? They try every chance they get to set you guys up with someone. Heck, papa gave some guy my number without me knowing and he called me a few weeks back. When I confronted him about it he said that the guy was a doctor and I should give him a chance. I told him that I have never seen the guy and don't know how he looks. He said that he could set up a meeting if that is what I wanted." Chike responded, "That is Uncle Emeka, always wheeling and dealing on everything from business to his kids." The four of them talked some more for the next two hours. As much fun as they were having it was getting late and the weekend was winding down.

Obi looked at his watch and said, "Dang it is 10:00 p.m. I need to start heading home and get ready for work tomorrow. He and Chike said their goodbyes to the family. Uncle Ugo said to Obi, "So what time will you be in the office tomorrow." Obi responded, "I should be in around 9 or10 a.m. I have a few things to handle before I come in." Ugo responded, "That is fine. I have a few things to run by you tomorrow." Obi enjoyed the perks of working for his uncle. He wasn't a stickler on time because he knew Obi produced and got his work done on time. Obi agreed to meet with Ugo and then he and Chike headed toward the car for the drive back to his place. On the drive back home, both of them talked about the conversation their mothers had with them. Chike said, "Both our mothers are strong on this marrying a Nigerian woman shit. It seems the older we get the more they talk about it. When I was a kid, they didn't care who we dated." Obi said, "Chike, they have always cared. They just never believed that we were ever serious with a non-Nigerian woman."

Obi asked Chike, "So does your father care if your wife is Nigerian?" Chike responded, "Papa, I think prefers it, but he ain't gung ho about the shit. I think he just wants the woman to be black. He is just more liberal about that issue. I know your dad is on that old school Nigerian shit." Obi responded, "Yeah, I am the oldest son and I need to marry a Nigerian woman to set the example for Chinwe and Okechukwu."

Chike posed a question, "If both women were equal would you be with a Naija or akata." Obi responded, "That is a trap question. In life, meeting two women with similar characteristics rarely happens." Chike said, "Nigga, this ain't a legal deposition. Just answer the damn question with a straight answer." Obi started laughing and said, "I have to be loyal to my Naija woman always. But I know I won't be with a Naija woman just for the sake of being with one just to satisfy my parents.

Chike laughingly said, "Well I guess I will take that answer as a yes. You always know how to play both sides of an argument. They must teach ya'll that the first day of law school." By the time they knew it they had reached Obi's place. Obi got out of the car and said goodbye to his cousin. As he walked into the house he started thinking about going back to work. He wasn't all that excited about going back to the boring ass grind of reading through business contracts. He felt he needed something different to do and would talk with his uncle about it during their meeting in the morning.

As he got on his computer to check his emails, he saw that he got a Facebook message from one of his law school friends. It was from his homegirl Nkechi Okoye. They were very close since his first year in law school. Nkechi wished him a happy birthday and asked what his plans were for the inauguration. She still lived in the D.C. area and told him that if he came up there he was more than welcome to crash at her place. She also let him know that she had tickets to the inauguration and possibly to a couple inaugural balls as well. Nkechi told him in the email not to procrastinate and buy his plane ticket as soon as possible. She knew he would wait until the last minute to get it. Obi had a smile on his face after reading that last sentence.

Nkechi knew Obi like the back of her hand. Obi at times wondered if he should have pursued something with Nkechi, but he felt their friendship was too good to jeopardize. After surfing the internet for another half hour, Obi took a shower and went to sleep. Awakened by his alarm clock; Obi proceeded to do his morning ritual. This consisted of watching CNN, listening to music, eating breakfast all the while getting prepared for work. Even though he had enjoyed his time off work, Obi knew it was time to get back into the grind.

His commute to work took him about 45 minutes from his house in southwest Houston to the office which was downtown. He usually went to work later to avoid traffic. When he arrived in the office, he made his usual rounds and greeted Miss Washington and Miss Jackson, who were the paralegals in the office. Both women were in the mid 40s and always wanted to know what was going on in Obi's dating life.

Miss Washington said, "Good morning, Obi and also happy belated birthday to you as well. I hope you enjoyed your time off." Obi responded, "Thank you very much ma'am. I am doing well. I think I enjoyed Obama's election victory a little too much."
"Obi, I am still on cloud nine about the whole thing, I still I have to pinch myself when I get up, just to make sure this really happened," said Miss Washington.

Miss Jackson came towards the area where Obi and Miss Washington were. Miss Jackson asked, "Hey, Obi how have you been doing? So are you still single or has anybody taken you off the market?" Obi laughed and said, "No ma'am, I am still available." Both women were always shocked by how a handsome, accomplished, man like Obi was still on the market. Miss Washington said to Obi, "I don't know what is up with this new generation of black women. They keep chasing these no good men who treat them like shit, but when a good brother like you comes around they don't want him."

Obi said, "I am not sure what they want Miss Washington." Both women were single and knew the struggles of finding a good man. They also felt that the African man was better than a regular black American man. Miss Jackson's daughter married a Nigerian man and she saw how he treated his daughter very well in comparison to black Americans." Miss Jackson said, "Don't feel bad sweetie.

Your culture raised you to be respectful towards a woman, which is something that many black people in this country don't do anymore. I know God will bless you with the right woman in your life."

Obi finished the conversation and headed to his office. When he got there, he saw that the office secretary, Nnenna left some messages on his desk. Nnenna was about 25-years-old, 5 feet 4 inches with brown skin, nice size breasts and booty. She was the only eye candy in the office. She was okay at her job, but Obi's uncle had hired her as more of a favor to one of his friends.

Obi's workday began with checking his emails and surfing the internet. He had a lot of work to get to after his time off. As he was getting into his work, he remembered about his scheduled meeting with Uncle Ugo for 10 a.m. He headed to Ugo's office and knocked on his door. Ugo opened the door and told him to come in and give him a few minutes to wrap up a phone call. As Obi came into his office, he noticed that his uncle had wasted no time in putting up a big Barack Obama poster in his office. Even the paralegals had gotten calendars of Obama and put up newspaper clippings of him in their offices. No one avoided expressing their political affiliations.

"So how is your morning going so far for you?" Ugo asked Obi after finishing up his phone call. "It's going well, Uncle, just trying to get back into the swing of things after my vacation and everything." Ugo agreed with him and said, "Well Obi the reason I wanted to meet with you is to see what your plans for your future are. I know that you have just turned 29 and probably are trying to assess what your next move will be."

Obi responded, "Well uncle I have appreciated the opportunity you gave me to work here for the last two years. I have thoroughly enjoyed my time here, but I feel like I want to do more. I remember when I was in law school; I hoped to do more to have an effect in helping with issues in the black community, particularly the inner city. I was hoping that maybe the firm could do some pro bono work with different community groups."

Ugo looked at Obi and said, "Obi I think what you are trying to do is great. But at this time the firm can't commit to doing anything like that. We are already understaffed and couldn't take on any more work, especially work not bringing in any money. But I still think you should pursue this on your own. I think so many people get in the law profession for the power and prestige, but I take the view of the great civil rights attorney, Charles Hamilton Houston. Attorney Houston described lawyers as either social engineers or parasites on society. Houston also determined that a social engineer was a highly skilled, perceptive, sensitive lawyer who understood the Constitution of the United States and explored its uses solving problems of local communities and bettering conditions of the underprivileged citizens."

Obi knew that his Uncle Ugo was right. If this was something he wanted to pursue, he had to do it on his own. Ugo was relieved that was all Obi wanted. He feared that Obi might want to jump into corporate law where the big money was at. He couldn't blame Obi if he made the jump. He was young, ambitious and had the world at his fingertips. Ugo knew that working for a small firm like his was good, but knew that corporate America could offer Obi new and bigger challenges. "Well Obi you know that you are free to use any supplies that you want. If you need any of my help in any capacity you know that I will always be available," Ugo said.

Obi thanked his uncle for everything and headed back to his office. Ugo sat and began to think about his own life. Ugo had come to the U.S. in 1968 at the age of 24 to attend college at Howard

University. He had come at a very contentious time in the country. The U.S. was escalating its involvement in the Vietnam War and the civil rights movement was coming to an end after the assassination of Dr. Martin Luther King Jr. The younger generation of black Americans, were frustrated with the lack of change they had been promised after passage of the 1964 Civil Rights and 1965 Voting Rights Bills. This coincided with the rise of the Black Power and Black Pride movement.

At first, Ugo wasn't too concerned with black American issues. He felt that he was a Nigerian student just trying to go to school and help his family back home. He and the other African students at predominately black Howard University felt like outsiders. Some black students would ask them why their great grandfathers sold their own people to the white man. Others would ask them if Africans lived in houses and wore clothes. Ugo and the other African students couldn't believe the ignorance they were hearing. They understood it from white people, but they felt like the black Americans were their brothers. But the black American students saw the Africans more as their opposition rather than their ally.

They felt the white man was giving scholarships to Africans to squelch the notion of racism. Ugo and the other African students felt that black Americans should be lucky to live in a country so rich and didn't see why they were so angry. The African students didn't realize they were just a pawn in the game that white people were playing with the Africans and black Americans. White people didn't think any more highly of Africans than they did of black Americans. But the main distinction is that most Africans weren't trying to disrupt the structure of America. By the late 1960s, most African countries had gained their independence and the African students wanted to go back and help build their countries after they graduated college.

White people knew that even though Africans and black Americans shared the same skin color, they didn't share the same goals. Ugo focused hard in his studies and graduated with his degree in engineering. His plan was always to go back to Nigeria after he finished school, but even though the Nigerian-Biafra War had come to an end; there was a lot of uncertainty in the country and he decided to stay in the U.S. He was able to find a few contract engineering jobs, but they only lasted for a few months and then he had to search for other projects to work on. By this point it was the mid 1970s in America, but black people still had a tough time finding work even with a college degree.-Ugo would question why he never got any jobs even though he had gotten work experience. He began to think that being black and Nigerian was hindering him. The situation in Nigeria was bad and it didn't seem like he could go home to stay for good. So with him being at a crossroads in his career, he decided to go to law school after two years of unsteady work. He thought that maybe adding more education to what he already had could help him out.

Ugo was still living in the Washington, D.C. area and decided to go to Howard for law school. As he had returned back to Howard, he had a new perspective about things. He had been going to hear black activists like Kwame Ture (Stokley Carmichael) talk about trying to unify the black race all across the world. While in law school, many of his classmates would explain to him about the history of black people in the country since the time of slavery. He began to realize that since he lived in the country he couldn't be oblivious to what was happening just because he wasn't an American.

During this time, Ugo began to reflect on the stories, his father, Ikechukwu, would tell about his grandfather, Chukwuemeka

48

Ifeanyi. Chukwuemeka was the Igwe (high chief) of Abagana and other surrounding villages in the late 19th century. He was a very fair but firm leader who treated his people well along with outsiders too. His people did business with other tribes in the region along with the British. Chukwuemeka didn't really trust the British and was always skeptical of their intentions. Those thoughts he had became reality as the British started to colonize Igboland. The British had given money to other chiefs to try and buy their allegiance and convince their people to as well.

The British knew that Chukwuemeka was one of the big time chiefs and getting his support was necessary to them. When they first came to Chukwuemeka he told them he would never talk any allegiance to any white man or woman. They continued for months in wooing him with large amounts of money and promises of influence in the government. Chukwuemeka would just laugh at them and said he couldn't be bought by them.

The British sent other chiefs to talk to him and see if that they could change his mind, but their efforts did little to change Chukwuemeka's mind. A few days after the chiefs had finished talking with Chukwuemeka; he got word from one of his advisers that the British were tired of his reluctance and were plotting to have some chiefs from surrounding villages attack him and his village. Chukwuemeka was shocked to hear of this supposed threat to him. He began to see the power that the white man possessed. He held a meeting with his advisers to decide on what strategy to take. All of his advisers said he should fight for his chiefdom. But when asked if he could win the fight, the advisers were reluctant to give him any assurance he could win. Chukwuemeka was now in his late fifties and suffering with declining health. He was in no position for a battle that would result in huge bloodshed of his people.

Chukwuemeka told his advisers that he would give up his chiefdom. They all objected to it, but Chukwuemeka knew his time had come. He told his advisers to put word to the other chiefs of him wanting to meet with them in a week. So the following week, all the chiefs gathered in Abagana to hear of Chukwuemeka's news. As he addressed his fellow chiefs, Chukwuemeka asked Chineke for strength and wisdom for all of them. He began by lashing out at the chiefs who had taken money from the British. He said that they sold out their people for a few pieces of gold coins and the white man's religion.

Chukwuemeka spoke about the plot that was conspired against him to remove him from his chiefdom. His anger turned into tears has he began describing how their villages had worked together for hundreds of years and how the white man could come so quickly and divide them. He said that the white man was the devil and would enslave the Igbos on their land. The other chiefs laughed off his prediction as that of a tired old man not wanting to see the times change. He finally said he would relinquish his chiefdom before deceiving his people into accepting the white man. With those words, the Ifeanyi family's reign had ended.

The other chiefs were shocked and puzzled by his actions; they felt the old man would fight to the end for his kingdom. But they were also relieved because most of the chiefs had great reverence for Chukwuemeka and didn't want to go to war with him. As the meeting ended and word spread of Chukwuemeka's leaving, the people of Abagana were saddened by him leaving their chiefdom. They were also happy that he decided not to engage them in a bloody war, which would have killed many people.

Even though he was no longer a chief, Chukwuemeka had the land that was passed on to him by his father. He started to do more farming and spending more time with his eight kids and two wives. Chukwuemeka still kept his eyes on what was going on with the British. But to his dismay, all of the forewarnings he told the chiefs a couple of years ago were coming to pass. He began to see Christian churches being built and some of the people in his village converting to Christianity. He also saw some of the men start wearing the British clothing as well. But there were two things that hit home to Chukwuemeka the most. First, he heard that the British schools were telling the village kids not to speak their native tongue. The white teachers said that Igbo wasn't a language.. Then he saw the people in his village start giving their kids English names. Some would make the English name their first name and the Igbo the middle or vice versa, while others gave up their Igbo last name altogether for English names.

Chukwuemeka couldn't understand why this was happening. In his mind, it seems that the white man had put some juju (curse) on his people to make them act the way they were. Even within his own household, he saw the influence of the British taking hold over time. He began to see his wives start to clamor for his younger kids to attend British schools and become Christians. Chukwuemeka even saw some of his older kids, especially his second oldest son, Ikechukwu want to work for the British. With all these changes happening so fast, Chukwuemeka fell into a deep depression and became very sick. The old man felt that he didn't recognize what was happening in his homeland. As his sickness continued to get worse, it seemed like Chukwuemeka was coming to the end of his life. He was barely eating anything and became very weak.

Out of desperation, his second wife, Uche, who had converted to Christianity, contacted a Catholic priest to their house to pray for her husband. Within a few days, the priest had come to Chukwuemeka's house. As the priest came to Chukwuemeka's house, he was escorted by Uche to Chukwuemeka's bedroom. When the priest entered the room, Chukwuemeka was lying on his bed and then rose up. "Who are you and what are you doing in my house?" Chukwuemeka asked. The priest said, "I am Father John and your wife asked me to come and pay you a visit." Chukwuemeka looked at his wife Uche sternly and began to cuss her out in Igbo for bringing this person into his house. The priest said to Chukwuemeka, "It looks like you are in your final days and you need to accept Jesus Christ as your Lord and savior before your die." Chukwuemeka looked at the priest and his wife then said, "I will never accept any Jesus Christ or accept the white man's foolish religion." The priest said, "I will continue to pray for your soul, but by not accepting Jesus Christ you will not be able to gain access to the gates of heaven, but you will be with the devil in hell."

Chukwuemeka who was very weak said to the priest, "I am already living in hell on Earth. You British people want to destroy the Igbo culture and replace it with yours. I will continue to pray to Chineke and my ancestors who have passed to defeat the white man."

After that Chukwuemeka told Uche to remove the priest from his house. As the priest left, Chukwuemeka asked Uche to have the native doctors come to see him. After a few days, the native doctors had arrived. They started by performing Igbo rituals to see if that would help. Then they told the family to sacrifice seven cows and fast to try and satisfy Chineke. After everything was tried,

Chukwuemeka's condition didn't change. Chukwuemeka started to realize that his days on the Earth were over. He was sad about not being able to finish raising his family and see them grow. Even in his weak state, he talked to his two oldest sons, Uzochukwu and Ikechukwu, about taking care of the family and his land. After a few more weeks of fighting, the great Chief Chukwuemeka Ifeanyi finally passed away. When the word got out of his death, all the chiefs from the surrounding villages came to Abagana for a two-day burial ritual for him. Even regular people who had heard of Chief Ifeanyi came to pay their respects to him.

A month after Chief Ifeanyi's death, his son, Ikechukwu had decided to head to the city of Port Harcourt and try and do some business. He had done a lot of trading with the British and was hoping to continue in the city. His oldest brother, Uzo, would stay in Abagana and look over their father's land. As Ikechukwu trekked to Port Harcourt, he had seen that his father's premonition had come true. The British had created a country called Nigeria by colonizing Igbos, Yorubas, Hausas, and other tribes. The British controlled all the businesses and deemed the people of Nigeria as uncivilized and savages who needed their help.

The Nigerians had no control of anything on their own land. Ikechukwu would see his fellow Igbos and the other tribes trying to get the most menial jobs that the British had to offer. A select few Nigerians were educated worked with the white man, but they never had any leadership roles. Ikechukwu stayed in Port Harcourt for six months, but finally went back to Abagana after facing the frustration of limited trading business opportunities.

As he went back home, he began to think about his father. Chukwuemeka's theory about the British enslaving the Igbo man on his own land had become a sad reality. Ugo started to link the struggle for the black man in America with that of the African man. During the mid 1970s, black Americans had used music and their afros to differentiate themselves from white culture. But while the Africans danced to their highlife music, the songs rarely discussed the issues facing their people.

It wasn't until Ugo heard a Nigerian musician named Fela Kuti, did he find someone articulating the African man's story. Fela was a Pan African along with being a human rights and political activist. Even though he was born and raised in a middle class family in Nigeria; he came to reject the Europeans' way of life. Fela's music fused the sounds of West African highlife and black American jazz with scorching rhetoric of black liberation and nationalism to create the musical genre called Afrobeat.

The song that Ugo heard from Fela that laid claim to this ideology was 'Gentleman', which had some of the most powerful lyrics that Ugo had ever heard. The song's hook or catch phrase was, "I no be gentleman at all ooo, I be African man original." The song said that Africans needed to stop copying the European's style and culture and embrace their own. In some respects, Ugo felt that Fela's music was the embodiment of stories about his grandfather. Many of his songs talked about Africans having a colonial mentality, how Christianity and Islam were money making organizations which had brought division amongst Africans, and he also talked about the issue of corruption in Africa that had become rampant after colonization ended in the late 1960s. Even though the Africans had gained their independence, they were now trapped in disarray, not by the Europeans but by their own people.

Ugo finished law school and was working in corporate

America, but he still listened to Fela to make him remember about the struggles of his people. As the years passed and Ugo married to Nkiru, along with having kids; he shared his love of Fela's music with his kids. He would always play his music in the house so his kids could soak up Fela's brilliance. The children were young and may not have understood Fela's words, but it was important for them to become familiar with the music. Later, it seemed that his kids never gravitated toward Fela's music, except Ugo's nephew, Obi did.

Ugo started reminiscing about how his nephew had grown into a man and he was happy that he had a hand influencing him. Ugo remembered how as a child; Obi would say, that Ugo was his second father. Deeply reflecting on the past; Ugo forgot that he wanted to discuss Obi's dating situation.

Ugo couldn't ask Obi too much the night before with Ugo's wife and sister-in-law dominating the discussion. Unlike Obi's father, Ugo was open to talk with his kids along with his nieces and nephews about their lives. Ugo called Obi's office and told him he would be coming. When Ugo arrived at Obi's office, Obi asked him, "So what did you wanna talk about uncle?" Ugo responded, "Well I forgot to ask how your dating life is going." Obi laughingly said to him, "Uncle, it's kind of stagnant right now. Tamika and I are still fooling around, but that is about it."

Ugo nodded his head and said, "Obi, I think you need to try and wean yourself from Tamika. She is a good woman, but you have to expand your search towards other women. I think you need to go to more young black and Nigerian professional association meetings. There will be some attractive single women for you to pick from." Obi told him he would look into going to the meetings. Ugo told Obi, "I know that it is hard coming to terms with turning 30-years-old and having your age passing by.

You need to have some balance to your life. It can't be all work or all play. Every man needs a good strong woman to help them along the journey of life. Your Aunt Nkiru believed in my dream of starting this law firm and paid a lot of the bills until I got everything up and going. I know you will achieve great things in your professional and personal life and I am just passing my words of wisdom to you."

Ugo finished the conversation with Obi and Obi thought about what his uncle said. He really didn't have any prospects beyond Tamika. He heard some people talking about the online dating thing, but Obi felt awkward about meeting someone from there. In his mind, Obi felt like he didn't have any problems approaching women and talking with them. His problem was having access to women and finding the right woman for him. He also knew that he had to find different avenues to meet women. Obi leaned toward the opportunity to go to Obama's inauguration. He knew it was farfetched that he would meet any women out there, but it was worth going just to be in the atmosphere of history. So, Obi sent a text message to Nkechi letting her know that he would be heading out there for the inauguration.

CHAPTER THREE

"So when are you going to come over here and get this pussy." That was the text message that Tamika had sent to Obi. It had now been six weeks since Obi decided to implement his new approach in dealing with her. He had taken Lamar's advice to just to have sex with her if that is the only thing that she wanted. For Obi it was hard to accept that his relationship with Tamika would only be as fuck buddies. But on the other hand it would at least give him some consistent pussy, which he was lacking at the moment. Even though Obi debated with himself about what he was doing with Tamika, he knew that most guys would revel in the situation that he had going on. It was rare to deal with a woman who just wanted sex and was okay with no commitment. Tamika was one of the few women who didn't have her emotions tied to her pussy. She felt that sex was just sex and nothing more than that. Tamika loved being in control and aggressive during sex, unlike most women who just laid back and didn't do anything.

When Obi first met Tamika in college, he thought she was just a tease who really wasn't fucking anybody. But after they started talking, he saw firsthand how high her sex drive was. It would be funny to see her be this polite, conservative woman around everyone else and later she would be giving Obi head in the car while he was driving. She was a true lady in the streets and a freak in the sheets. Up to the point that he had started dating her, Obi's sex life was pretty mediocre. Obi never really dated any women who truly liked having sex a lot. Obi was always told by everyone how some good pussy could fuck your head up. He always felt that he was too mentally strong to have that happen to him. But Tamika changed his notion of that very quickly. As much as he didn't want to admit it early on, Tamika had him pussy whipped. She would sometimes withhold sex from him to try and control him.

It seemed that what she was doing worked early in their relationship, but after one year Obi had broken her pussy spell on him. When that; Tamika felt that her sex game was the only advantage she had over him. She knew that she couldn't keep Obi interested mentally for a long period of time. For the first time in her life, Tamika had to make a guy interested in her beyond her good looks and great sex. Tamika also knew that Obi would be going to law school at Howard and would probably meet many women with whom he would be more compatible. She decided to break up with him first to save herself from him doing it to her. She told Obi that she didn't want to do a long distance relationship above Obi's insistence that he could make it work.

Obi finally responded to her text message, "I'll be there in an hour to tear that pussy up like I always do." As Obi was driving to head to Tamika's place, he started thinking about his dating situation. Even though it was cool just getting ass from Tamika, he knew that the shit wouldn't last forever. He had yet to follow his uncle's advice or try doing the online dating thing. As much as he didn't want to admit it, Obi couldn't imagine Tamika not being in his life. He began to hold out faint hope that what they were doing would somehow make her reflect on their situation and change her mind. He was still pondering what he would do even as he had pulled up to her place and called her to let her know that he was outside. As he was walking up to her door, Obi began to think that having sex with Tamika wasn't letting him move forward with his dating life. He knew that he couldn't really give any woman a real chance while he was still fucking a woman he still had feelings for. But as soon as he knocked on the door and she came out with only a towel on and looking sexy as hell, those thoughts disappeared.

Obi and Tamika had sex like they always did for an intense 30 to 45 minutes. "I can't believe we are doing this," Tamika said. Obi responded, "What are you talking about?" Tamika said, "I never thought you would be okay with us just fucking. This doesn't seem like the Obi that I know." Obi laughed at her comment and said, "I have grown up a little bit since we were in college. I'm just giving you what you want. This is what you want right?" Tamika said in a hesitant voice, "Well yeah this is what I want."

Obi was hoping for her to break down and profess that she loved him and wanted them to get back together. But that never happened and Obi responded, "Well there it is." As Obi got out of her bed, he started to get dressed. Tamika looked at him and said, "So where are you going?" Obi responded, "Well I was going to head back home since we are done having sex." Tamika started to get really anxious. Even though she was just having sex with Obi; she wasn't ready to let him out of her life either. She was still trying to figure out what she wanted to do and was trying to keep Obi at bay until she made a final decision. She knew she still had a piece of Obi's heart and still played on that emotion with him. "Why don't you stay and I can cook you some food and then we can watch some movies as well." Obi wanted to make Tamika feel like she was just a booty call. But as much as he wanted to play the coldhearted nigga role, the nice guy in him wouldn't let himself dog Tamika out like that. So Obi stayed with Tamika and they cuddled on her sofa for the rest of the evening. Obi wasn't sure what Tamika was up to, but he was happy to be with her.

When Obi left Tamika's place the next morning, he began to think that maybe her wanting him to stay meant that she was looking for more than just sex. Obi jumped to the conclusion that maybe this was a small sign things might be changing between them. Once he got back home he turned on CNN to catch the news for the morning. The media was still discussing how Obama was going about the business of putting his cabinet together. There was still the intrigue to see if Hillary Clinton would be in his administration after her tough primary race with Obama. On the outset, it seemed like she didn't want to be in his administration. But after several talks from Obama and others, she accepted the position of Secretary of State.

In any normal post election transition, this selection would have been very big news. But with the thought of a long recession and even a depression looming, who Obama would select as his economic advisers was the hot topic of debate. Many of Obama's liberal supporters wanted him to pick people who would champion economic policies for the working and middle class since they weren't helped by President Bush's policies. People felt that the Bush administration was too closely tied to Wall Street and the agenda they prescribed contributed to the recession. To the dismay of Obi and others, Obama caved in and picked Tim Geithner as his Secretary of Treasury. He was the head of the New York Federal Reserve and was in charge of regulating the big banks, which had crippled the U.S. financial system. Obama also selected advisers who had been working for the major banks as well. In Obi's eyes he knew that Obama was picking these guys because he was told you have to pick safe people who would give confidence to the stock market because it had been free falling since mid September.

Obi began to feel that Obama's mantra of change was coming undone as he added a lot of people to his cabinet who were also part of former President Clinton's administration. Obi still hoped that since Obama was running the show; he would direct his cabinet on dealing with the issues he campaigned on and *not* avoid confrontation to gain re-election in 2012. It seemed with Obama in the White House and the Democrats controlling both Houses of Congress by huge margins, that the sky was the limit in terms of how ambitious they could be in their legislative achievements.

While Obi was watching TV, a commercial came on for an online dating site. Obi started laughing as he saw the advertisement and began to think this might be a sign for him to join. He went to his computer and pulled up the online dating website. As Obi checked out the website he said to himself; "Well, I'll give this shit a chance, I ain't got nothing to lose." He started setting up his profile and adding some pictures. After doing all of that, Obi saw of the matches that the system had generated for him based on the questions he had answered. It surprised him to see the amount of fine ass women that were on the site. Obi like most men always felt that the most attractive women had a plethora of dudes trying to mess with them. But as he was reading their profiles, the women had faced the same situation as Obi did. Most of them just didn't have much access to meeting people beyond going to the clubs. He started sending messages for a response to different women that he had some interest in.

After being on the site for about an hour and a half; Obi finally logged off. He felt that these women on the site were actually serious about dating since they paid a monthly fee for access to the website. This made Obi overly confident that online dating would give him a nice rotation of prospects to choose from. He also felt that he could tell his friends about the new source to meet women.

Obi was listening to some music when he got a call on his cell phone. It was his friend, Lamar. "What's up my nigga; what is going on with you?" Lamar asked. Obi responded, "I'm doing good man, just at the crib chilling." Lamar and Obi had talked a few times since his birthday, but all of the conversations were brief. Obi still hadn't got a response from Lamar about going to D.C. for the inauguration. Obi had already bought his plane ticket and wanted Lamar to come, but he felt that dude was a grown ass man and if he wanted to go he would be more proactive about it. Lamar said, "That's good man, so what's up with you and Tamika?" Obi responded, "I took your advice and I've just been having sex with her. She seems fine with the arrangement. After we finished having sex last night, she was trying to be all lovey dovey with a nigga. She didn't want me to leave and just wanted to watch movies and cuddle with me."

There was a long pause in the conversation and then Lamar said, "Oh, that's what's up." Obi jumped in and said, "I think Tamika might want to get back with me. I got a sixth sense about this shit though, Lamar. When I was getting out of bed and putting on my clothes, she got all glossy eyes on me. She was also hesitant when I asked her if all she wanted from me was just sex." Lamar let out a big sigh and said, "Obi, what are you talking about? I know you still cut for Tamika, but I think you letting fucking interfere with your thought process. Tamika is a woman that you dated for three years, so for her to be emotional one time after the both of ya'll had sex doesn't mean she is trying to get back with you. Even if you give her the benefit of the doubt that she does wanna get back with you; has she verbally communicated this with you at all? For all you know, she could be talking to another dude."

Obi said, "I don't think Tamika is talking to anyone else, even if she is, she never mentioned it to me." Lamar responded, "Obi, you are smart dude, but one of the most gullible people I know. You gotta get this image of Tamika you had when she was in undergrad out your head. She is a grown ass woman right now. Why would she tell you she is messing with another dude? She might be trying to decide between you and another dude. These women are scandalous as hell and I would never put anything past them. All I am saying is that I don't want you to hold out hope that she will just be jumping back in your arms anytime soon. If I could be totally honest with you; if she really wanted to get back with you, wouldn't she be with you right now."

Obi began to digest what Lamar said and he couldn't fully accept that Tamika didn't want to be with him. Obi always believed that outside factors like him going to law school in D.C. was one of the reasons why they weren't together. He also believed that Tamika was older now and that she would have a better understanding and appreciation for the type of man he currently was. Obi was also a very logical and quantitative person; he believed if someone had all the evidence showing them facts that were undisputed that the decision for that person to make would be very obvious and crystal clear. Obi had accepted that his friendship with Lamar had changed since their time in college.

Regarding Tamika, Obi hadn't come to terms with the ending of this chapter in his life and was prolonging the inevitable out of a sense of nostalgia and not wanting to accept the unknown. The other thing for Obi to contend with is that women seemed to base their decisions more on emotions than on logic. Obi grew tired of talking about Tamika and decided to change the subject with Lamar. "You won't guess what I joined today," Obi said. Lamar couldn't guess. Obi finally said, "I joined an online dating site this afternoon." Lamar started laughing and said, "Damn, nigga I know you are having a hard time meeting some females, but this takes the cake. I didn't know that you were this desperate." Obi said to him, "I knew you would say some shit like that. I have to admit I was hesitant about the whole thing, but decided to see what it is about. But real talk; they got some nice looking women on there. I don't know if they talking about anything, but it is another outlet to meet some more women." Lamar responded, "Well dude you try it out and let me know about it." The both of them ended their conversation without Lamar bringing up his intentions about going to D.C. Obi started to think about how much he had grown since his early years in college.

When he first entered college in 1998 he was a blank slate who was pretty much defined by his height and was searching to find his place on the campus. Obi was looking to join some school-based organizations. He was drawn to the black Greek fraternities like a lot of other black students were. Obi didn't know anyone who was in fraternity or sorority at the time. At first glance, Obi saw them as the guys on campus that threw parties and had women around them. But as he started to inquire more about the frats, he learned that they did a lot of positive things on campus and in the community. During the first semester of sophomore year, one of the frats that he was interested in had a meeting for prospects.

During the meeting the current members of the frat talked about the famous men who were part of the organization and that they wanted to bring in high character individuals to the fraternity. They discussed the networking opportunities that the frat could bring during and after graduation. While Obi was there he talked to some of the members and ran into a few Nigerians who were part of the organization. Once he left the meeting, he was even more excited about the chance to be in the fraternity. But as Obi started trying to gather details about getting into the organization, he began to be less enamored with it. Even though the members of the frat said they were a non-hazing fraternity, he heard from other people that the pledging process involved getting your ass whopped for six to eight weeks while you were on line.

It was ironic that the so-called black intellectuals in college did the same thing as dudes trying to get into a gang on the streets. Obi would also hear how frat members would talk about how tough they were while on line because of the amount of physical abuse they took. In Obi's mind, the frats were representing themselves as helping black men grow during their time in college, but were okay with beating and sometimes killing one another all in the name of brotherhood. Obi started to realize that the black fraternities and sororities were giving off this image of black elitism. The organizations made young black men and women believe that they more authentically black than other non-Greek black students. They gave this illusion that while pledging; you learned some secret information about black history that only people in the organization would know about. In reality most men and women who finished pledging only learned the Greek alphabets and history about their organization.

The other disturbing thing was how skin complexion and physical appearance played a role of the people picked to join one of the organizations. If a woman was light skin and considered attractive she was perceived to be in one particular sorority, while a dark skin man with glasses was pegged to be in a certain fraternity. This showed Obi that even black Greek organizations were subject to the confused identity crisis that affected many black Americans. He also saw how the Greek organizations had a conformist attitude toward things and he realized he didn't want to be a part of that. By his junior year he started to become more of an individual. He decided he wanted to go to law school and was more focused on getting himself ready for that. Obi also became more socially and politically conscience of what was happening in Houston along with events around the world. He wanted to have a purpose beyond finishing college and getting a job.

Obi's eyes were opened even more at an event presented by one of the black fraternities. The event discussed the life of the Lynn Eusan. Obi only knew that there was a park on campus named in her honor, but he thought she was just a white woman who had donated some money to the school. He was surprised to hear that the woman was the first black homecoming queen at the University of Houston in 1968 along with being a social and political activist. Obi listened as her friends described the struggles of black students at the university shortly after the school integrated in the early 1960s. They talked about how committed Lynn was to demanding that black students at the university were treated better and had equal rights. She and others were instrumental in getting the University of Houston to have an African American Studies Program. Even though she was killed tragically in 1971, her former friends and classmates still showed deep love and reverence for her. In Obi's mind, he saw how people his age at the time did so much for the future generation of black students at the school. One of the speakers spoke about how the black students used to have parties in the same place that the event was being held and how they had a sense of camaraderie in those days, which he thought was missing in the current generation.

Obi reflected on comments the speaker made. Obi saw the lack of social advocacy among the black students. He would go to different forums held by the African American Studies with barely 10 people in attendance. But when there was a frat party going on, you could get droves of people to come and then some. Obi wasn't against partying, because he had done his fair share like everyone else. He just didn't know why some black people couldn't show at least a little more interest for things that affected their community. An example of this was when the African American Studies program was trying to organize a rally of students to push the dean of the liberal arts college to hire a black man to become the new chairman of the program. The man was one of the finalists for the position. The students wanted the administration to hire him because he wanted to transform African American Studies from a minor to a major field of study.

During the rally, the students in the program were trying to get petitions signed so they could take it to the administration to show that there was an interest in people wanting to major in African American Studies. As the rally was happening, one black male student approached the group to see what the purpose of what they were doing was. When one of the organizers of the rally told the student what was taking place; the student started laughing. He told them that it would be foolish to waste their time and money in getting a degree in a field that had no job opportunities.

While this conversation was taking place, a group of Pan Africans who came to show support overheard what was going on. One of the women in the group came over to thank the student organizers for what they were trying to do. The woman then looked at the student who was arguing with organizers. She told him, "My dear brother, the white man has brainwashed you. He has you believing there is no value in knowing about your people. The problem is that he has trapped you and a lot of our other brothers and sisters in a box. I believe all black students should have an African American Studies degree along with another degree in their field of choice." The student asked, "Why?"

The woman said, "My brother if you can combine your knowledge of finance, engineering, or any other major with knowing the history of your people; you can help build back up our communities. I know that many of you have been bred to get your degrees, find a job, move to the suburbs, and forget about the struggle of your people. Your generation has to realize that people struggled through blood, sweat, and tears for you to have the opportunities that you share today. It is time for you to carry the torch, try, and advance our cause as far as you can. Don't sit on the sidelines and just be a bystander to the injustices that continue to face our people on a daily basis."

Obi and many other students listened to the woman and for

some it was the first time they had been challenged to do anything for their people. It was easy for them to be active on campus about black issues, but they might not have the same fervor after they graduated. In the college environment you are encouraged to find yourself and search for your passion, but in the world outside of college you are told to conform to the standards of society. For many black students including Obi, the first time they were exposed to being socially and politically aware was not through the stories of the Civil Rights Movement, but ironically enough through watching the TV show called 'A Different World'.

When his family first moved to the United States, Obi remembers watching 'The Cosby Show' and 'A Different World' on Thursday nights all of the time with his family. Even though he liked both shows, 'A Different World' was his favorite of the two because it dealt with young black students in college. The show was a spin-off of the Cosby Show, which portrayed the Huxtables' second oldest daughter, Denise, attending the fictitious Hillman College. The show was America's first weekly look at black college students at a historically black college. 'A Different World' dealt with the regular lifestyles that affected most college students; ranging from trying to pledge a fraternity to students' financial struggles.

The show didn't just deal with the stereotypical portrayal of college life that was common in most white TV shows and movies. It covered topics like racial identity, gender, and economic issues in the black community. Additional topics included opposition to the First Gulf War, apartheid in South Africa, and the legitimacy of black colleges and universities. The show brought together students from different socio-economic backgrounds along with their different perspectives on life at the Hillman campus. The true genius of the show was that the school demanded excellence from students on the first day they arrived to the school. It was more than just getting an education through reading textbooks and taking tests.

They showed that everyone from a professor to the owner of the restaurant in the student center could offer an introspective look into life. The show followed in the tradition of historical black colleges and universities to make their students into leaders and advocates in their communities by shaping their minds. You also got to see the progression of the characters from their freshman year to graduation. You witnessed the evolution of the students and saw how they tackled the real world of life beyond college socially and professionally. The show was credited for fueling resurgence in black cultural nationalism in the mid 90s and led to a huge uptick in enrollment of students to historical black colleges. Even though the show ended a few years before Obi started college, it gave him a prequel to black college life.

When Obi finally was at U of H and watched reruns of the show, he was astonished how relevant the show was and how it mirrored some aspects of his college life even though he didn't attend a historical black college. It was funny how he came across certain people who reminded him of the characters from the show. For Obi, the character who he thought personified himself was Dwayne Wayne. Many of his friends also made the same observation. Obi didn't mind the comparison because he thought the character was a smart, average dude who was cool because he was just being himself. It didn't matter to the character, if he was the only one who thought his flip up glasses were cool; along with his limited swag among campus women. Although, not as smooth as some; the character was able to charm the popular and attractive Whitley Gilbert. They eventually fell in love.

In Obi's relationship with Tamika; he sometimes felt that their situation mirrored Dwayne and Whitley's. Obi finally stopped his daydreaming of his college years and began to think about how he was going to make an impact in the community. Since his meeting with his uncle a few weeks back; he was still brainstorming how he wanted to tackle the various problems in the black community. He began to think maybe it would be best to get involved in some community groups and then determine the actual need. He researched and wrote ideas down then took a break to watch television.

He started flipping the channels and came across TV One where they were playing some old episodes of Martin and The Fresh Prince of Bel-Air. Obi was always overjoyed when he saw those shows and countless others from the 1990s. In Obi's mind, that era was the golden age of black television where the shows had good writers, characters, and plots that were entertaining and were at times thought provoking. It seemed that since that time, these type of black TV shows had become a thing of the past and now were replaced with a bunch of reality shows and subpar TV shows. These shows played on the buffoonery and stereotypes of black culture and weren't good in Obi's eyes. But the crazy part was that a lot of black people were watching these shows.

Obi began to wonder if people were actually watching these shows from boredom or if there was a paradigm shift with black people and their views toward good television. Obi felt that shows from his childhood through high school days wouldn't be embraced and watched by a lot of black viewers today. He wondered if a character like Dwayne Wayne would be a leading black male character on a TV show in this fake celebrity world that black people seemed to want to be a part of. His character would probably have to be transformed into an athlete, along with being in a fraternity and finally he would be a ladies' man with a lot of swag to go with it. Obi also saw how the same things were going on with black movies. He remembered watching classic black movies like 'Love Jones', 'The Best Man', and others during the 1990s. The movies painted a picture of black people as having the same everyday issues of every other racial group, but they added their own spin and culture to it. During the 1990s, the writing, directing, and characters on many shows were on point.

It seemed during the mid 2000s, black movies started to take a turn for the worse. Certain movies like 'Soul Plane' and 'First Sunday' lacked creativity, depth, and played to the worse stereotypes of black culture. Obi couldn't deny that the 1990s didn't produce stereotypical movies and TV shows, but it just seems that today things are more stereotypical. Obi wondered about clownish perceptions and acceptance of limited quality black roles in movies. . Obi started to grow tired of black television and stereotypical movie roles and became interested in another genre of movies.

Obi remembered being in high school and seeing his father watching some VHS tapes of Nigerian movies that he had bought back from his trips to Nigeria.

The video quality was terrible and the acting wasn't much better either. Even though Obi and his siblings didn't care to watch the movies, his parents along with his uncle and aunt would be glued to the TV watching it for hours at a time on the weekends. Obi's parents encouraged the children to watch the movies so they would continue to know their culture and not become akatas.

It is said that when you live in another man's country, that man was only going to show his culture and way of life to that person. The movies gave Obi's parents a reprieve from American culture if not for only a couple of hours and also told stories about their former lives in Nigeria. Unlike American movies, the Nigerian movies were very spiritual as well as cultural. By the time Obi started going to law school; the Nigerian movie industry had become so expansive it was now referred to as Nollywood. Nigeria had become the second biggest movie making industry in the world behind India. It was astonishing how the Nigerian film industry was built in less than 20 years by filmmakers with limited financial resources and no real training in the field of cinematography. Unlike the U.S. model which shows most of the new films at the theatre; in Nigeria because of the lack of economics for most of its people; that strategy couldn't work. So what happens with most Nigerian movies is they go straight to DVD after filming. This helped make movies more accessible to Nigerians and allowed Nollywood to expand all over the world, including other African countries.

Obi sometimes wondered why black Americans didn't think in the same manner as Nigerians. He felt that black Americans had more access to better film equipment and the knowledge of the film industry, but they still were waiting for someone to make or put them in movies. Obi felt that black Americans were always mad when a black actor/actress was overlooked for an award.

The problem is that black people wanted to get acceptance from a white population who didn't know or care about their culture. It was always ironic how Hollywood would make movies without thinking about black people at all. Obi felt that black Americans needed to tap into the continent of Africa which had a population of almost one billion people. With hip-hop and rap being huge over there, it wouldn't take too long for the black American film industry to make big strides in Africa as well. Sadly, most black Americans still had no clue regarding potential access and money that Africa has to offer. Some black Americans still carry the stereotypes of Africans that the white man bestowed on them in the early 20th century.

As Obi began to wind down his evening, he began to get sleepy. It seemed with all the TV watching and daydreaming, he hadn't finished his brainstorming of ideas he was working on. He decided he would get back to it later on in the week.

Unfortunately, for Obi the next few weeks were busy with finishing up year-end deadlines for work and getting ready to celebrate Christmas.. He decided he would put off his brainstorming projects until the beginning of the New Year. One thing that he didn't put on hold was his pursuit of women, specifically online dating. When he first set up his profile, he didn't get a lot of responses, but not long after that; his in box started to fill up with women showing interest. Obi started to feel that he had hit a gold mine with unlimited potential. He responded to the women that he liked and they exchanged numbers and talked over the phone with them. For the first time in his life, Obi felt kind of like a playa of sorts.

He was going on dates almost every other day of the week with different women. But after going on his first round of dates with the various women, Obi's enthusiasm began to wane. It seemed that most of the women weren't looking for a man, but rather they wanted a placeholder instead. Obi began to realize that the women were drawn to him by his job title as a lawyer, but whenever he would talk briefly about what he was doing at work; the women would become disinterested.

Obi also saw that the women had portrayed various interests

on their profile, but quite honestly he realized that many of them just added stuff to make themselves sound more interesting than they actually were. . In his mind, online dating was like a prospective employer finding someone's job resume on Monster.com or Careerbuilder.com. The candidate looked good on paper and even dressed the part on the interview, but at times when the questions and probing time came; the person was really an empty suit.

Obi felt that he had to go back to the drawing board in regards to the dating game. He thought that maybe he could meet someone new at the end of the year and see what would happen in 2009. Obi also felt that dating someone else would possibly take his mind off of Tamika.. In Obi's mind, he felt that he would be closing the year in the same manner that he would be bringing in a new one; with a lot of doubt and uncertainty in regards to his future.

CHAPTER FOUR

"Five, four, three, two, one;, Happy New Year, everyone!" The TV announcer said. Obi and his family brought in the New Year together at home like they always did. As everyone in the room was tipping their glasses filled with champagne and wishing each other a prosperous 2009; Obi was digesting the whole moment. He was entering his last year in his twenties and in his head the countdown to his 30th birthday started clicking. Obi played down the significance of the milestone to everyone as just another birthday, but to him it was a big deal

Obi contemplated his year at hand and the New Year also marked three weeks until the United States would have a black president with his family occupying the White House. Even though his election victory was two months ago, the buzz and excitement was still in the air. It was estimated that almost two million people would ascend on Washington D.C. for Obama's inauguration with millions more watching on TV and the Internet around the world. This inauguration seemed like it would be the biggest global event in world history. It was even more ironic that Martin Luther King's birthday would be observed a day before Obama would be sworn in. There was also the coincidence of Obama accepting the Democratic Party's nomination 45 years to the day that Dr. King gave his 'I have a Dream', speech in Washington, D.C.

Obi and others felt that this was some type of divine thing that God designed for this particular time in the history of man on this planet. As Obi was sending out massive Happy New Year text messages to friends and family, he saw that Tamika had sent him a message as well. Chike had come over to him and said, "Happy New Year, Obi. So what are your resolutions for this year?" Obi laughed and said, "Chike, I don't believe that you get a whole new slate just because the year changes. People think that switching the year really makes a big difference with things." Chike responded, "You are right my cousin, but it is also true that we may need to cut old habits or even let some people go out of our lives as well." Obi took the comment that he needed to deal with the Tamika situation once and for all this year. It seemed that every time he wanted to end it, the both of them would have sex and he just pushed the issue further down the line. Nevertheless, Obi knew that with work at the law firm, doing his seasonal tax work, and the inauguration on his plate for the early part of 2009; he would be busy and didn't want to imagine the thought of not having some consistent pussy around him.

He also wanted to seriously start putting his plan together for working with black community groups as well. Unfortunately, that wouldn't be something he could kick in gear because of his prior commitments. It seemed that with 2009 not even a couple hours old;

Obi still wasn't going to face his main objectives for this year. The next few weeks into 2009 would be busy for Obi. He was going to have almost a week off to go to the inauguration and he had to do a lot of work so he wouldn't be too far behind when he got back.

Even though Obi hated working longer hours and taking work home, it would be all worth it in the end. Obi had decided early to get his ticket to fly out to D.C. on the Friday before the inauguration. He wanted to beat the hectic sea of people who would be arriving at Ronald Reagan Airport. He finally finished all his work on Wednesday and then used Thursday to rest and pack for the trip. Obi went to the store to buy some more winter clothes, because even though the weather in Houston was around 60 degrees; that would all change once he got to D.C. The forecast was slated for mid to high 20 degrees.. It seemed that of all the elements of D.C. that Obi did miss, the brutally cold winters wasn't one of them.

On Friday, Obi arrived at the airport and didn't relax until he was actually on the plane. He survived a tough few weeks, but now it was time to focus on his trip. Obi sent a text message before the plane took off to his law school friend, Nnamdi Okafor, to let him know what time to meet him at Reagan Airport. Obi was excited to get the opportunity to see Nnamdi and Nkechi again. The two of them were the most influential people that he had met in his life; beyond his Uncle Ugo.

Obi thought about back in the day when he moved to D.C. and it was in the campus bookstore that he bumped into Nnamdi. They were both looking for a book for the same class. The two started talking about the class and about how much the book cost. The conversation led to the fact that they were from the same village of Abagana.. It seemed liked they were old friends as they continued to laugh and talk for a couple of hours. Phone numbers were exchanged and Obi was excited about the whole situation because he didn't know anyone in D. C. during that time. Obi was extremely happy to meet someone from his hometown.

Obi found out that Nnamdi was three years older than him. Nnamdi's ' family moved to the States when he was two years old, but they went back to Nigeria regularly to visit. Nnamdi got his bachelor's degree in engineering and wanted to be a patent lawyer. He had a couple years of work experience before he came to law school. While Nnamdi had his situation lined up for him; he saw that Obi was very ambitious but was still trying to piece together exactly what he wanted to do in law school. "So why did you decide to go to law school?" Nnamdi asked Obi while they were eating lunch one day. Obi answered, "Well I want to use law to help black people." Nnamdi asked, "Okay, so in what capacity do you want to do that?" Obi was silent for awhile and tried to think about a good answer. Nnamdi jumped in and said, "Obi, you have to be more definitive in what you are trying to do here. This isn't like being in college; where you weren't sure what you wanted to do. You mentioned before that your uncle is a lawyer and he always encouraged you towards the profession.

But you have to do this for yourself and nobody else. You don't want to be one of those people who gets out of here in three years and doesn't know what to do with their law degree. There are already way too many people doing that and I know you don't want to join that list."

Nnamdi and Obi had the same younger and older brother relationship that Obi had with Chike when they were kids. Obi respected Nnamdi because he always had his best interest at heart even when his commentary was very blunt. Eventually, Obi shared the issues regarding Tamika with Nnamdi and how the relationship had been over for just a couple of weeks. Unfortunately, Obi didn't have any time to think about it much back then because he was focused on moving to D.C.

Nnamdi felt that Obi should let Tamika go for the most part. He didn't think that Obi knew the amount of power he had by being a young, black man in law school at Howard. He would always remind Obi that this might be the place for him to find the right woman.. Nnamdi would always say to Obi, "Even though these women are here for school, they are also looking for a potential husband.. You have to know that you are always being watched. If a woman runs into you up here; it ain't by accident, it is by design." This notion became more self evident about half way through Obi's first semester at Howard.

Obi went to the library one day to gather some information and while there he saw a woman that was in his contract law class. She was 5 foot 6 inches, had a beautiful dark complexion,, with a slim build, and had shoulder length wavy hair. .

Obi tried not to be too obvious, but he didn't know how to just glance and look away. Finally the woman noticed that Obi kept looking at her and then approached him. The woman said to him in a sensual voice, "You don't have to be afraid to come speak to me, I won't bite." Obi laughed at the comment and said, "I don't know what you are talking about." The woman responded, "Dude, you have been checking me out for the last five to ten minutes. Even my home girls noticed that you were looking. You do look familiar; I think you are in my contract law class."

Obi tried to play if off by saying, "Yeah I have seen you a couple of times." The woman got a little cocky and said to him, "Dude I see you and your other friend looking at the all the females in the class. You guys need to keep your eyes in them books and stop chasing ass." After that they broke into laughter.   The woman finally said, "Well let's formally introduce ourselves to one another, my name is Nkechi and what is yours?" Obi responded, "My name is Obinna and my friend's name is Nnamdi." Nkechi said, "I should have known the both of you were Nigerian. We are all over the place." The conversation continued toward class and then switched to their personal lives.

Nkechi Okoye was born in the United States and her parents were from the village of Ogidi in Nigeria. She decided to go to law school because she wanted to go into corporate law. Nkechi had majored in finance in undergrad like Obi. She also wanted to work in the black community to try and deal with the issues of poverty and economic inequalities in all facets of society. Nkechi was currently doing some small workshops on financial literacy at the community center on campus for students and local residents. She told Obi how she wanted to work with residents in low income housing units. In various cases; slum landlords were usually not up to date on fixing certain building code violations.

Obi was very impressed with how Nkechi was detailed in her plans for her professional career. Their conversation went on for about 30 minutes and then Nkechi finally asked Obi a question. "So when are you going to exchange numbers with me?" The statement caught Obi off guard; he wasn't sure if she wanted him to holla at her or just wanted to study together. Before Obi could say a word, Nkechi told him with a smile, "Don't get all excited and stuff, I ain't trying to talk to you. I'm just looking to maybe study with you and your friend." Obi tried to play it off cool like that was the same conclusion he had come to. "I knew that's why you wanted it; I was just trying to see what you were talking about." Nkechi laughed at the notion and said, "Obi, don't try that reverse psychology bullshit on me. We both know that you want to get at me. But don't worry I won't put you in the friend zone yet."

They both took down each other's contact information and said their goodbyes. Once Obi got home he called Nnamdi and told him what transpired at the library. Nnamdi had also become his go to person on women the same way Lamar was for him in undergrad. The difference was that Nnamdi gave a more thought out and in-depth analysis of situations; unlike Lamar's shoot from the hip approach.

"Well I think she is interested in you man, but she is trying to see how you are going to act. I think the three of us studying will help you have a better shot to get to know her. Like I said before; these women are looking for a husband. But they are trying to see what you are about before they let their guards down. Even if it doesn't lead to anything, she is a good person to know. After we all finish law school, you have to have a good network of people around you. That is something that black people aren't good at. We got people who can get you into a club, but rarely know someone who can get you into an interview. I saw this first hand in my previous jobs; it is not about what you know but who you know."

Obi took heed to Nnamdi's words about dealing with Nkechi. Even though there was some intrigue into what Nkechi was about; he still had feelings for Tamika. They still talked on the phone about twice a week. He talked to her about coming up to visit him and held out hope that they would get back together in the future. But Obi also knew he had to focus 100 percent on school and knew he couldn't maintain   a long distance relationship.

Nnamdi, Nkechi, and Obi started studying with each other on a regular basis. During the course of their studying, they would have a lot of side conversations and it seemed the three of them started to gel with one another very quickly. They explored everything that D.C. had to offer which consisted of going to hear Tavis Smiley, Cornel West, and other political and social leaders give speeches on campus. The three of them also went to the U.S. Supreme Court to hear some cases, and enjoyed the social scene in D.C. during their free time.

They also had a ritual of watching the Sunday morning news shows and would later meet up at someone's place to discuss the topics of that day. If it was during football season, they would gather to watch the games for a good part of the day. As the years passed, the three of them became very close friends. Nnamdi finally got into a relationship, so he didn't hang with the group as much. It took some time but it was finally just Nkechi and Obi by themselves. Obi always had a deep respect and admiration of Nkechi. She had a very big influence on his law school experience. Nkechi saw his talents and didn't want to see it go to waste. She challenged and encouraged him to be more involved with issues in the community. Nkechi would always tell Obi, "You have to make your own legacy in this world, like all the great men and women before you have done." The two of them never got into a relationship. They flirted with each other frequently, but nothing ever materialized. Obi really wanted to be with her, but at the time Nkechi was so focused on achieving her post law school goals, that she didn't have time for anything serious.

Nnamdi referred to Nkechi and Obi, as the characters of Harper Stewart and Jordan Armstrong from their favorite movie, 'The Best

Man'. Those characters were portrayed as never getting with each other in college, even though they liked each other. Nkechi and Obi would always laugh at the comparison, but in their minds they knew it was true.

As the pilot announced that the plane would land in D.C. within approximately 10 minutes, Obi snapped back to the present and wondered how his trip would play out. Once Obi got off the plane and went to get his luggage from baggage claim, he saw Nnamdi standing at the arrival gate. "My nigga Zik, what's been going on with you?" Obi said. Obi and Nkechi called him that after Nnamdi told them that his parents named him after the first president of Nigeria after their independence from Britain, Nnamdi Azikiwe. He is the only Igbo to ever hold that position since that point. Nnamdi responded, "I'm doing well. I have just been fighting with all the congestion in the city because of the inauguration. I have never seen D.C. this fired up before. It will be an interesting weekend needless to say."

The two men left the airport to meet with Nkechi.

"Obi, it feels surreal that in less than four days a black man will be the President of the United States.. I'm still in a dream world about the idea of this actually happening. Anyway how have you been doing man? I know this is the last full year in your 20s. How are you feeling about turning 30?" Obi responded, "Yeah man I feel that same sentiment as well. I remember waking up the day after the election with an extra swagger in my step. I think all of us black people have felt like it's been Christmas since Obama won the election and it seems that the inauguration will cap off the almost two month celebration. In regards to your second question; I guess I'm good. It's just another milestone to mark down in my life, no big deal."

Nnamdi shook his head and said, "So what do you think about

Michelle Obama? She looks good for a 45-year-old woman." Obi responded, "I can't lie. If my wife is in anywhere close to the shape she is in at her age; I would be happy. I have a small crush on her as well. If she was the same age as me, I would have given Barack a run for his money." Nnamdi started laughing and said, "Don't let anyone hear you say that. The next thing you know Secret Service will be coming to take you away. So what's up with the women that you actually have a chance of getting with?" Obi told him that he wasn't messing with anybody at the moment. Nnamdi persisted and asked him if there was anyone he was just fucking. Obi lied to him and told him that he wasn't. "Nigga, why the hell are you lying to me right now?" Nnamdi asked Obi. Obi tried to look surprised that Nnamdi was challenging him. "What are you talking about Zik? I'm telling you the truth."

Nnamdi said, "Obi I know you are still fucking Tamika. That shit is written all over your face dude." Obi finally confessed that he was and then asked Nnamdi how he knew he wasn't telling the truth. "Obi, you have always been a bad liar. I noticed that every time you lie to someone that you never look them directly in the eyes. Also I know that ya'll were bound to fuck a couple of times." Obi started to explain to him the whole situation with Tamika. "Honestly, we really just started fucking again on my birthday. Since then it's been pretty much an almost weekly thing with us." Nnamdi said, "I ain't trying to judge you man. But what are you trying to get out of the deal? We both know that fucking can only last for so long until somebody wants something more. Where do you fit in this equation?"

Obi reluctantly said, "Zik, I honestly don't know what is going on. I would like to get back with her, but she hasn't even made any mention of us going toward that direction." Nnamdi said, "All I can say is; don't get in too deep that the pussy outweighs your priority to be in a relationship with her or another woman. So have you been pursuing anyone beyond Tamika?"

Obi said, "Man, this dating shit gets harder the older you get. I have resorted to do the online dating thing and maybe running into some women while I am up here this weekend. But anyway enough about my problems; how are things at your job?" Nnamdi was currently working as a patent lawyer for a technology company in Arlington, Virginia about an hour and a half outside of D.C.

Nnamdi responded, "It is going okay; this recession is kind of slowing things down right now. I just hope that we make it through this year and they don't have to go through any layoffs." Nnamdi didn't feel like dwelling on that situation and decided to switch the conversation back to dating. Nnamdi said, "I think that women have a sense of too much entitlement when it comes to dating. I always felt when I was still dating that the man on a date with a woman was like the court jester with the king and queen. The court jester had to be a comedian, intellectual, and do whatever it took to keep the royals entertained. In my eyes, I feel that is the same thing a man has to do when he is on a date with a woman. The results are the same, the royals and the woman just sit back and do nothing and at the end decide what happens from then on out."

Obi was shaking his head in agreement with everything that Nnamdi said. Obi said, "Zik, you took the words out of my mouth. That is what your boy has been going through lately. These black women are always saying that niggas ain't shit and that there aren't any good black men." Nnamdi responded, "It is funny you said that statement. My girlfriend's friends are always saying that bullshit now. But the more I think about it this issue has been dominating in the news lately. I remember watching that CNN documentary Black in America and saw how some black women say they have to resort to dating white men because of the lack of quality black men to choose from. In my opinion, this whole matter just makes me laugh. The problem for some these women is that they are finding bullshit men is because they ain't about shit and they don't know what they want for themselves. Let me ask you something. Do you seem to get bored after you finish talking to some women?" Obi told him that was the case. Nnamdi asked a follow up question. "So do you know the reason why you are bored and uninterested?"

Obi responded, "Because they don't have too much to say about anything." Nnamdi said, "The reason that is so, is because they are educated but not smart." Obi jumped in and said, "Zik, what are you talking about? These women went to college and have jobs." Nnamdi said, "That is my point, Obi. Most people who go to college just memorize stuff to take a test. They never really learn the material for anything beyond that purpose. If you think back to undergrad, how many people did you know that were engaged about a particular issue and could talk about it with some critical analysis?" Obi said, "Honestly, I didn't really know anyone that did that." Nnamdi said, "Okay so now let's go back to dating. If someone doesn't know what qualities they want in a person; they just fall back on generic answers like wanting someone who is smart, funny, interesting, and all that other bullshit. People usually just want a girlfriend or a boyfriend."

Obi asked, "Isn't that what everyone should be striving to have." Nnamdi responded, "Yeah, as a teenager and in your early 20s. In reality a girlfriend or boyfriend is a person who takes up your time. That person is fun to be around for awhile. The problem is that in most adult relationships, this is what is usually going on.. You should be striving to be looking for a partner. This person adds value to your life and is an equal investor in the relationship. The both of you will be growing together along with challenging one another to become the best each other can be." Nnamdi added another comment, "Obi, when is the last time a woman told you she liked you because you were a genius. I want to bet that nobody ever told you that ever in your life before. That is the problem I have with black women, they are always talking out of both sides of their mouths. These women swear up and down that they want to date a nice normal guy that treats them good, but the minute that guy is put in their face they start saying that is not what they want."

Obi asked Nnamdi, "So what do you think all these black women coming down for this inauguration are looking for?" Nnamdi responded, "They are looking to meet their own Barack Obama. The problem is; that type of man has been in their face all the time, he just didn't look the way they wanted him to look. I saw pictures of Barack when he was our age, that dude wasn't a ladies' man by no stretch of the imagination. So what will most likely happen is some of these women will meet a guy who looks and dresses the part and will be all excited about that. By the time they realize the dude ain't about shit, they are all in love with him." Obi sighed hearing this analysis by Nnamdi.

Nnamdi said, "So Obi you thought you were going to come here and meet your own Michelle Obama or something." Obi played it off and said, "Nah Zik, I was just trying to get your account about the situation." Nnamdi laughed and said, "You are lying your ass off Obi, you thought you were going to meet your dream woman out here. If I was you; I would focus my attention on trying to get with Nkechi." Obi looked at him and said, "Nkechi and I are just friends and that is all to that situation." Nnamdi said, "Obi let's cut the bullshit man. You cut for her real hard back in the day, but she wasn't looking for a serious relationship. But I gotta be 100 with you; she was real giddy about you coming up here this weekend. You know Chi Chi tries to be calm and cool all the time, but I think she knows that she fucked up with you back in school. I always said that ya'll are like Harper and Jordan from the 'Best Man'. The only difference is that you don't have a girlfriend to worry about."

Obi jokingly said, "Since you want to assign people characters from that movie, then I guess you were their lame ass friend, Murch. But on a serious note man, I always thought Nkechi was the woman for me, but wasn't sure if she wanted to break away from her career for anybody. But I never knew how things would work out with the distance and everything." Nnamdi said, "I know that she ain't too happy with her job and was talking about doing something else. Anyway just see how the weekend goes before you start thinking too far down the road. The two of you will be alone for a couple of nights at her place, so that should be time to have a discussion about what is really up with you guys. I consider the both of you guys my brother and sister and I know that the both of ya'll are definitely on the same wave length. You know that she is on that black power to the people movement like you are on and she also can have fun and joke around just as well. I hate to be sappy about the whole thing, but she might be what you have been looking for."

As Nnamdi was calling Nkechi to let her know that he and Obi were down the street from her place, Obi began to revisit his feelings that he had for Nkechi. He always used the friendship card in regards to her so that he wouldn't get hurt if something between them didn't work out. But now at this point of his life, he was ready to make a leap of faith and see what the future might have in store for them.

After a long drive and terrible traffic, Nnamdi and Obi finally reached Nikechi's place. As the both of them exited from the car, Nnamdi reiterated to Obi what they had discussed earlier about Nkechi. Before they could reach Nkechi's townhouse, she was outside waiting for them to come. "Damn Chi Chi, it is cold than a muthafucka out here, why are you standing outside?" Nnamdi asked. Nkechi replied, "My place is kinda of hidden, so I didn't want you guys to get lost looking for it." Nnamdi and Nkechi gave each other a hug and then Nkechi and Obi embraced and gave each other a very tight and intimate hug. "It is good to see you Obi, it has been a minute since we have seen each other last," Nkechi said.

Obi and Nkechi continued flirting with each other until Nnamdi broke in sarcastically saying, "Harper and Jordan, can we take this love fest inside. I am not trying to catch pneumonia messing around with the both of you." The three of them walked into the house. Once they got into the house, Nkechi took off her coat and Obi realized that Chi Chi looked different. In school, she was very slim without too much of a body, but now she got a little bit thicker and her booty got bigger as well. Nkechi had went with a natural hair style and was wearing some stylish black framed glasses. She had evolved into a grown and sophisticated woman in the last couple of years. Her townhouse was full of Afro centric artwork and sculptures. Nkechi asked Obi, "So how was your flight?" Obi responded, "It was good. When you are on a long flight it gives you a chance to do a lot of reflecting." Nkechi asked, "So what were you thinking about?" Obi said, "I guess, just about the whole inauguration and how we three met during law school. I can't believe it has been five years since we all started school together." Nkechi responded, "Yeah, Obi it doesn't seem like that long ago either, but time does fly for real though. So how is everything going with you at the law firm?" "It is good, just doing contracts and taxes for these small businesses. You and Zik got the interesting jobs working in corporate America."

"I don't know about all that, it pays the bills I guess," said Nkechi.

Nkechi was currently working as a corporate tax attorney for a big telecommunications company. She had been there since she graduated from law school, but was for the most part bored with the job. Obi asked her, "So Chi Chi, what is the problem with your job?" Nkechi responded, "It just ain't that fulfilling. I didn't go to law school to find legal tax loopholes to make sure big companies can keep their huge billion dollar profits. If you also throw in the 60 to 70 hour work weeks and it just seems like when I'm at home I just eat and sleep."

Nnamdi said, "Well that is how things are though for you Chi Chi. I work somewhat similar hours. But I can't complain, this is what I signed up for and want to do as well." Nkechi said, "Well, Nnamdi you always wanted to chase that corporate ladder shit. I am not knocking it, but the lifestyle is definitely not for me. To be honest; I have also started to question if I still want to be a lawyer anymore." Obi asked Nkechi, "So what is it that you want to do?" Nkechi replied, "I am looking at probably going back to school and getting my Masters in Urban Policy. I have already started sending my applications in to start school in the fall." Nnamdi looked at Nkechi in disbelief about the whole situation. Obi for the most part was surprised but not shocked. He knew that Nkechi was a free spirit who wasn't too much into the conformist culture of corporate America. Instead of pursuing her dreams of working in social advocacy, she succumbed to her parents' pressure to pursue corporate law. Her parents warned her that she wouldn't be able to feed herself by working for the poor and disadvantaged.

Nkechi thought she could still do her financial literacy seminar once or twice a month, but when the demands of her job became too great she was unable to continue. She had been battling with trying to satisfy her parents and society's perception of what she should do versus her own desires and dreams. Finally, it seems that she decided to take a stand and do what she wanted to do. After the long silence, Obi said to her, "Hey Chi Chi, I think what you are doing is great." You only have one life, so do what makes you feel good." Nnamdi jumped in and said, "Well Chi Chi, I think you are making the wrong decision, but it's your life so do with it as you feel." Nkechi felt that Nnamdi's comment was condescending and said, "Look Zik, not everybody wants to follow the American way or really the Eurocentric view of what constitutes a good life." Nnamdi said, "I just don't want to see you throw away three years and over $100,000 in tuition, so you can try and help people who don't even want to help themselves. This isn't law school Nkechi; that trying to save the world bullshit doesn't get you too far anymore."

Nkechi responded, "Zik, I see that the white man has got you believing you have a real stake in their company. Let's see, as the economy continues to tumble if you won't be the first person to be let go. We don't mean anything to the companies we work at. We are just some black faces to meet their diversity quota." Obi could sense the tension between Nnamdi and Nkechi was building and he decided it was time to cool down the conversation. "The both of guys need to chill out for a minute. Zik, this is Nkechi's decision and she didn't ask for our commentary, so let's give the conversation a rest."

Nnamdi said, "I am okay with my sister's decision. She knows that I love her deeply. Sometimes I come across as an overprotective brother, but that is only because I care about her. I apologize if I came across as to abrasive."

Nkechi said jokingly, "I don't know why you apologized; you already know we are going to have some more disagreements this weekend. You know when the three of us are around, our sibling rivalry continues. Since I am the only girl; I have to have tough skin when I am debating with you guys." The three of them started to talk about their plans for the evening. "I want to check out this new reggae club that just opened up. I know it is going to be jumping tonight with every one coming into town for the inauguration." Nkechi said. They agreed that was what they wanted to do. Nnamdi decided to leave because he had to go back home to change and then pick up his girlfriend. Once Nnamdi finally left, Nkechi and Obi started to catch up about other issues. Nkechi asked, "So are you still talking to that silly akata girl you were dating in college?" Obi answered, "If you are referring to Tamika, the answer is no. We talk here and there, but for the most part we are pretty much just friends."

Obi didn't like lying to Nkechi, but he couldn't tell her he was still fucking Tamika and then try and talk to her as well. That would surely be a recipe of disaster. Nkechi was secretly happy that Obi wasn't talking with Tamika. She also felt that this was finally their chance after all the time had passed since law school. Obi asked, "So why do you care if we are talking or not?" Nkechi responded, "I don't really care who you are talking to; I was just trying to see if you had any one special in your life." Obi began to think that Nkechi was trying to position herself to see what he was doing, so he decided to throw some questions at her. "So are you talking to anybody right now?"

"Well at the moment I am single as hell. I couldn't tell you the last time I have been on a date; I know it has been at least six months." Nkechi said. "Damn, Chi Chi what has been going on with you?" Obi said. "Like I told you and Zik earlier, this job has been consuming my life. I just don't really have that much time to go out and socialize. Along with that; I just haven't really been meeting too many guys that I am interested in." Obi laughed, "With all these black guys in D.C., I thought you would be able to find at least one dude that would be a good fit for you."

Nkechi responded, "You would think, but that's not the case. I mean some of these black men have this huge ego and think they are God's gift to women since they are college educated with professional jobs. I don't have a problem with someone being proud of their accomplishments, but it doesn't mean I will be on your dick just because of it. Then you got the potential dudes who are the starving artists and writers. These guys are fun to hang around with and also have an interesting perspective on life. . But a lot of them usually don't have a steady job and usually don't have any money to actually date a woman. I respect their love for what they want to do, but I think they have to act like a grown man and be more responsible. I am 30-years-old and need a man who I can see myself marrying and that involves someone who can bring some reasonable level of financial stability to the table. I'm not saying he has to make more than me, but he can't rely on me to pay all the bills."

Obi nodded in agreement with Nkechi's comments and said, "I guess the dating game is hard on men and women. I know my dating situation has been not been too good as well. I told Zik that I resorted to trying online dating." Nkechi said, "I know that online dating is the new thing to do right now. I know it's easy and convenient, but I am still old fashion when it comes to meeting people. I always think that the first initial contact with someone is very important for me. I am usually good at reading someone and seeing if we got a good vibe or not. Also I think that people believe they will find a man or woman that will be different then a person you meet at a bar or club. Unfortunately, the same people are using both avenues to try and find someone." Obi said, "Yeah I had to find out about how that worked the hard way. I think everyone is looking for the fast and easy way to compatibility, but I realized that there is no sure fire way to get there. ."

Obi and Nkechi were pretty open with each other about everything including their sex lives. Obi asked, "So I guess since you haven't been dating that also equates to no sex as well, right?" Nkechi laughed and said, "You would be correct about that. I just use my vibrator to get me though the rough times." Nkechi started to think how she would be able to keep her hormones in check with Obi staying with her. She had used her vibrator almost every day in the morning before work and before she went to sleep at night. Nkechi was due for some sex and wouldn't mind doing it with Obi, but she didn't want to jump the gun and possibly send some mixed signals about what she wanted from him. Nkechi could feel her pussy getting wet and decided it was time to end the conversation about sex. "That's enough now, about my sex life or lack thereof one. I am about to get some rest before we go out tonight," Nkechi said.

"I made you some rice with stew and chicken so you just have to go into the kitchen to get it." Nkechi went to her bedroom to take a nap. While Obi was eating his food, he thought how none of the women he was meeting could stack up to Nkechi. He was biased because he knew her for some time, but she was always keeping it real about herself. She never was on some bullshit and he thought at this point of her life she knew what she wanted for herself and what type of man she was going to be with. He also knew that by Nkechi putting herself out there about her dating life, she was telling him that if he wants to try and pursue something that she would be open to the idea..

For Obi it was funny how the woman he thought he would meet out here was staying a room away from him. As he finished eating, Obi got a text message from Tamika. She was asking him if he had got to D.C. safely and also about how he was doing. He responded to her that everything was going well with him and he would talk with her once he got back to Houston in a couple of days. Obi knew he had to get more clarity about Nkechi before he could start thinking about turning the page on his situation with Tamika. Obi would be lying to himself to say he didn't have any feelings for Tamika regardless of how much more compatible Nkechi was for him. Obi decided to get some sleep after his plane flight and after conversing with Zik and Nkechi for the last couple of hours. He knew he would be doing a lot of moving around the next few days and needed to get all the rest he could.

After a couple hours of sleep Obi woke up and was looking for Nkechi to see when they would be heading out to the club. Once Obi got to the living room he saw that Nkechi, Nnamdi, and Nnamdi's girlfriend, Ogechi were already dressed and ready to go. "There goes sleepy head, damn Obi you was knocked out for the past three hours. We tried waking you up but you weren't budging. We was about to give one last try before we were just going to head out without you." Nnamdi said. Obi responded, "I apologize everyone, give me about

30 minutes to shower up and dress and then we can make moves after that." Everyone was cool with that and Obi quickly got ready to go. They all decided to take one car to the club so no one would get lost trying to follow someone with all the traffic going on in the city.

"It's going to be fired up tonight ya'll. I hope everyone is ready to have fun and get their dance on. I know I am ready it's been a minute since I have partied and especially with my best buddies." Nkechi said. Obi said, "Ok Chi Chi, I am going to get you on that dance floor and see what you are working with." Everyone started laughing and Nkechi said, "Obi, I hope you got a lot of rest this evening, because I am definitely going to break you off." Ogechi said, "Ya'll don't have nothing on me and Nnamdi." Obi and Nkechi started laughing and Obi said, "Ogechi, your man can't dance to save his life and I don't know if he can hang with this reggae shit." Nnamdi jumped in and said, "I see we got some haters in the car; that's cool I will have to show ya'll. I'll just let my dancing do the talking for me." Ogechi said, "I see ya'll talk shit to each other to almost everything." Nkechi said, "Yeah that is what we do. We make fun of each other all the time. If the three of us get together, we definitely are going to be going hard on each other."

Driving through the city, Obi started to get nostalgic seeing all the spots and landmarks of D.C. Even though he loved being in Houston; it was D.C. that always had his heart. While the other three were continuing their conversation, Obi was silent as he was just taking in everything. He saw the pictures of Obama and his family posted on almost every street corner in the city. Nnamdi asked him, "Obi, are you good man?" Obi responded, "Yeah man, I'm just thinking about how much I miss being in the city and also being around ya'll. I wouldn't want to be celebrating this moment in time with anybody else but ya'll." Nkechi said, "Don't get too sentimental on us Obi, we going to have time for all that later. Right now I am ready to get my party on."

The four of them finally arrived in downtown D.C. after a 30 minute drive. Even though it was only 10 p.m.; the club had a line going into the streets. Nnamdi said, "We got here at the decent time and we are still going to have to wait for a minute to get in." Ogechi said, "Babe, don't worry about it, you tried your best in driving here and taking some side streets. We are just going to have to wait for awhile, no biggie."

As the four of them exited the car, Ogechi and Nkechi were walking in front, while Nnamdi and Obi were behind them. "So have you gotten a feel for what Chi Chi is talking about?" Nnamdi said. "Obi responded, "Yeah, she was doing some prodding to see if I had anything going on with anybody. She asked about Tamika, but I just lied to her when she wanted to know if we were fucking or not." Nnamdi said, "Okay man you played if off cool. Nkechi is cool but you can't tell her about that." Obi said, "Yeah, you are right man. She told me she ain't been fucking anybody for awhile. I don't know whether to believe her or not." Nnamdi said, "She ain't fucking anybody man. I remember Ogechi told me the subject came up with them and Chi Chi told her she wasn't going to be fucking until she got into a serious relationship."

Obi said, "Okay that's what's up. If I wasn't trying to get at Chi Chi I definitely would be hollering at some females because I see all types of ass heading to this club." Nnamdi said, "How do you think I feel. I can't look too hard or Ogechi will be getting into my shit. She already knows I like big booties, so I gotta look but don't touch tonight." Obi asked, "So what is up with you and Ogechi, how long have ya'll been dating." Nnamdi answered, "We have known each other for about a year, but we just started getting serious about six months ago. It's cool for now; we are just going with the flow." Obi asked, "That is good Zik, do you think she is the one." Nnamdi responded, "Obi, you know I don't believe in that whole idea. I think there are a lot of women in the world I could be compatible with. For the time being; me and her are occupying each other's space."

Obi said, "Dang Zik, I see you getting all philosophical on a nigga. I have to agree with you on your assessment. I think that the way a soul mate is portrayed in movies and books is so romanticized. Even if you do find your soul mate; it doesn't mean that will be the person you marry and stay with for the rest of your life." The four of them finally reached the front of the club and waited in line for about one hour to get into the spot. The club wasn't very big, but it was wired up from wall to wall. The music was blaring and everyone was sweating from all the dancing going on. Before they were going to hit the dance floor, the four of them headed to the bar to get some drinks. Obi ordered two shots of Patron for everyone and they all toasted to a great weekend of celebrating.

After they got some more drinks, Nkechi grabbed Obi's hand and took him to the dance floor. As they were approaching the dance floor the DJ stopped playing the music. Everyone in the spot thought that maybe the club was going to get closed down for being too crowded. After about 10 minutes of waiting, the DJ announced that reggae singers Beenie Man and Sean Paul would be coming to the stage to perform some of their songs.

The club goers were ecstatic. Nkechi looked at Obi and smiled and told him, "I hope you are ready because I am going to throw this ass on you; let's see if you can handle it. If you hadn't noticed it has gotten a little bigger since the last time you have seen me."

Obi said, "I see you are talking a little noise, but I will be the judge of how good you are." As the performances started, Obi could tell that Nkechi wasn't playing around. He was trying to keep up with her, but Nkechi was going extra hard on him. After some time, Obi decided to just stand and let her do her thing as she rubbed her booty all over his jeans.

Obi could feel that his dick was getting really hard and Nkechi noticed it as well. She whispered in his hear, "I can tell that I am making you very excited from my dancing. I can stop if you can't hang anymore." Obi said, "Nah don't stop, you are doing your thing. I will catch up with you." Nnamdi and Ogechi saw the both of them dancing and came up to them. Ogechi said to Nkechi, "Damn girl you are working him out for real." The both of them stopped dancing for awhile to take a breath and then Ogechi and Nkechi went to the bathroom.

Nnamdi started laughing at Obi and said, "Both of ya'll were dancing pretty intensely. It looked like ya'll was damn near fucking on the dance floor." Obi responded, "You ain't lying about that, I think it was the combination of the alcohol and some pent up sexual yearning on her account." Nnamdi said, "I know one thing I hope you got some energy left, because I think ya'll might be fucking by the end of the night."

Obi asked Nnamdi, "Yeah I was thinking that is where things might end up. Do you think, us having sex would complicate what we are trying to do?" Nnamdi responded, "That is a good question, even though ya'll are pretty close; we all know that sex does change stuff. I think you should just go with whatever she wants. If she is insisting on ya'll doing it, then you are a man and should go for it. If you turn her down, she might think that you aren't interested in her like that."

Nkechi and Ogechi returned from the bathroom. Obi could take one look at Nkechi and he knew that all the drinking had taken its toll on her. Ogechi said, "Nkechi is pretty messed up, she was throwing up in the bathroom." Nnamdi said, "Well I guess the party is over." The four of them left the club and started walking back to the car. As soon as they got to the car, Nkechi jumped right inside and went right to sleep. On the car ride back home, Nnamdi and Ogechi had noticed that Nkechi was lying on Obi's shoulder while she was still sleeping.

Nnamdi said, "Aww, don't both of them look so cute back there together. We need to take a picture of this moment, so ya'll can share it forever." Obi said, "I see you with the jokes, Zik. This ain't fun, she is breathing on me and it smells like a mix of vomit and alcohol." Nnamdi responded, "Dude you need to stop complaining, you are so much into that girl you would drink her bath water."

They finally arrived at Nkechi's place where Obi helped her get out of the car. Obi said, "Zik, thanks again for the driving man. You and Ogechi, be careful driving home and I will call you tomorrow; so we can try and meet up. Obi helped Nkechi get into her apartment and walked her to her bedroom. Nkechi started coming around and asked, "Where am I at?" Obi said, "We are back at your place. You had too much to drink and we left early." Nkechi said in a slurred speech, "I am sorry, I hope I didn't mess up your time. Did you enjoy yourself tonight?" Obi said, "I had a great time hanging out with you. We will talk about everything in the morning." Nkechi agreed and changed out of her clothes and went to sleep. Obi went back to his bedroom. In his mind he thought that he didn't have to worry about having sex with Nkechi tonight. But it did make him wonder if tonight would have been his best opportunity for something to go down between the both of them.

CHAPTER FIVE

Obi woke up with a slight hangover from all the previous night's drinking.

He decided he would make breakfast for .both him and Nkechi. As he finished making the food and began to eat, Nkechi came into the kitchen. "Damn my head is hurting. I was partying and drinking way too hard last night," Nkechi said. Obi responded, "Yeah you were, but it was all good though. Everyone has one of those nights." Nkechi said, "I don't remember too much from last night, but I do remember dancing my ass off and wearing you out on that dance floor." Obi said, "I think you are flattering yourself, I was holding my own with you." Nkechi laughed and said, "Obi please, you were holding on my waist to keep yourself from falling. I told you that you couldn't hang with me." Obi asked, "Well anyway, what are the plans for today?" Nkechi said, "I don't know yet. The weather is still cold as hell, so I ain't trying to make too many trips outside if I don't have to."

Obi agreed with her assessment.

Nkechi said, "We need to catch up about current events. I know we didn't have much time to talk about things since you got into town yesterday. So what do you think about the whole Tavis Smiley versus Obama debate about Obama having to be accountable to black people?" Obi responded, "I think that Tavis does have a point about the whole matter. I think that he has been getting unfairly criticized by black people because of his critique of Obama. All that Tavis wanted to know; is if the Obama administration will have a black agenda to address the problems that face our community."

Nkechi said, "I agree with you on that. Black people have to distinguish between Barack Obama, the historic figure and celebrity from the president who still will be leading a country that often throws black people's issues under the rug. I have already heard a lot of black people saying that because he will be inheriting two wars and now a terrible economic situation that we should wait until he possibly gets a second term for him to properly address our concerns. That to me is the most self deflating shit I have heard of in my life. It seems that this was the same rhetoric that black people said when President Clinton won in 1992 after we gave him damn near 92 percent of our vote. Everybody said he would take care of us in his second term. Unfortunately, the Democrats lost their majority of Congress in 1994 and he still managed to win reelection in 1996. But once the Monica Lewinsky scandal hit in 1998, he was trying to save himself from being thrown out of office."

Obi responded, "Yeah history is a muthafucka isn't it? Now the new mantra they feeding us is that Obama is the President of all of America, not just black people. Even though we carried him in the primaries against Hillary Clinton and gave him 95percent of the vote in the general election. They make it out like we are too dumb to understand that Obama can't just take money from the Federal Reserve and pass it out to all the black people in the country."

Nkechi said, "That is the slave mentality that a lot of black Americans still carry with them. They are happy to get whatever hand me downs that white people will give them. Even though they followed the electoral process and voted for their guy and he won; they feel scared to ask for their issues to be discussed. Politicians promise to do a lot of things of the different constituencies that they represent. Obama told gay people he would end 'Don't Ask, Don't Tell' in the military. He told the labor unions he would fight for them to continue their collective bargaining rights and he told Jewish people that the U.S. would always protect and work in the interests of the country of Israel. I think the problem is that black people don't have any network or movement to push their political agenda."

Obi said, "I don't know what you mean; explain that comment to me in more detail." Nkechi said, "Okay I will. I think that the real genius of the Obama campaign was that they changed the way people organized around issues. The centralized approach that dominated the civil rights movement from its inception is no longer effective in the era of social media and blogs. Their grassroots movement empowered the people and made them feel like they were a part of the campaign. It seemed that the need for the traditional black leaders in getting out the black vote diminished as well. When you have a smooth speaking charismatic man like Obama along with a lot black entertainers on his bandwagon, there was no doubt that the voter turnout for black people would be extremely high as it was. But unfortunately, Obama's ascension has exposed a big glaring problem. Now that we have a black man as the president of the country, who within the black community would dare challenge him about dealing with their issues?"

Obi began to think about what Nkechi was talking about. He responded, "I guess nobody will try and do it." Nkechi said, "You damn right nobody would or they will be ostracized like Tavis was. Obama got all of the black–owned radio stations and magazines twirled around his finger. You know they all want to have access to him and his family so they will just toss softball questions to him so he won't alienate them in the future. I think it would be safe to call Obama, the black Don Corleone from The Godfather movie."

Obi started to laugh and said, "Chi Chi you are crazy for real. But I think that your point is well taken. It is funny to see how white liberals have built up their movement since 2004. I remember watching the election between Bush versus Kerry and it seemed like the Democrats were pretty much spineless against the attacks thrown at Kerry from the Republicans. But it seemed like they have changed their approach since then. The left wing of the Democratic Party has become very influential by starting blogs and websites like The Huffington Post, Moveon.org, and the Daily Kos which weren't even around in the last election. Now they have become a huge voice for Democrats.

You also can't underestimate the role the cable television station MSNBC played in the elections. You had people like Keith Olbermann and his colleagues taking on the Republicans on every smear or the twisting of facts they made about Obama. It was good to see them actually call out other media outlets for letting assertions like Obama not being born in the U.S. or of him accused of being Muslim just fester to bring interest and to increase their ratings."

Nkechi responded, "Yeah that is true, but I know one thing;

those liberal blogs and MSNBC will still keep the heat on Obama when they feel he isn't lining up on the issues they are supporting. I don't always agree with all their stances, but those liberals don't fuck around and they mean business."

Obi said, "Yeah but what scares me is that black Americans will just sit back on auto pilot and just assume Obama will take care of their issues. For many black people, voting is the only time we are involved in any form of political discourse and we have to be dragged kicking and screaming to do that process. It is amazing that even though we vote in high numbers, that most black people just select the candidate that has been picked for us. We don't have our own public policy institutes or think tanks to develop any actual policies addressing our community issues."

Nkechi responded, "You are very dead on with your assessment Obi. It is like white people are telling black people that you guys need to let us handle the complex stuff and just vote for us and we will take care of ya'll. They will even throw us a black man or woman candidate to have us believe that person is running the campaign, when in truth whites are controlling everything. But to their credit, besides civil rights, black people have no real signature issues to bring to the table."

Obi said, "It is sad for me to hear you say that, but you are right. But I think even if we move beyond the issues, these liberal groups help raise millions of dollars for these candidates during election time. These politicians only represent the interests of the people who donated the most money to their campaign. Unfortunately, black people aren't giving enough money to have their interests being represented. That is the bleak reality that faces black people. Just when we learn how the game works, the rules are changed and you have to adjust on the fly."

Nkechi said, "I have really enjoyed this conversation, but enough with politics for right now. I am about to take a shower and get ready for the day." As Nkechi went to take a shower, Obi decided to call Nnamdi and see what was going with him. "Zik what is good with you man?" Obi asked as Nnamdi picked up the phone. Nnamdi responded, "I doing well my man. Just trying to get myself together after the long night we had." Obi said, "Yeah I feel that. I just finished eating breakfast with Chi Chi." Nnamdi said, "Oh okay, so did the both of ya'll have sex last night?" Obi responded, "It didn't go down last night Zik. Once she got into the house, she went straight to her bed and went to right to sleep. She really didn't remember what had taken place earlier in the evening." Nnamdi said, "Dang man, it seemed like things were trending in that direction toward ya'll doing something last night. But too much alcohol does mess things up all the time."

Obi responded, "Yeah you are right about that. I am not really that worried about the whole thing. I kind of was reluctant in the both of us doing anything in the first place. Maybe we not having sex; is a sign that I need to take things slow with her." Nnamdi agreed with him and said, "Well I will be over at her place in about an hour for us chill out and then we can decide any movements after that."

Obi began to think about how he and Nkechi would talk to each other and about how they felt for one another. It had seemed that they were dancing around that issue and each person was waiting for the other to make the first move. Obi knew that Nkechi would never truly come out and say how she felt about him. She would just continue overtly flirting with him as a sign that she was interested. In the past, Obi took the flirting as nothing but playfulness on her part, but after their conversation from yesterday and their intimate dancing the night before, Nkechi was showing her vulnerability and willingness to profess her affection for him. Obi decided to not worry too much about his situation with Nkechi. The both of them would be around each other for the next week or so and that would give him enough time to find a way for them to talk about their feelings for one another.

Obi went to the bathroom in his bedroom and took a shower and got ready for Nnamdi to come over. By the time Obi had finished up, Nkechi was in the living room and Nnamdi had arrived to her place just a short time before. "So I see you have recovered from last night Chi Chi. You was drunk as hell along with working your boy out on the dance floor," Nnamdi said to Nkechi.

Nkechi responded, "Yeah Obi told me about everything that happened this morning during breakfast. It has been awhile since I have been that out of control with myself. If I didn't wake up with a hangover and a bad headache, I wouldn't have complained too much about it. It is like I told ya'll yesterday; this job doesn't give me the chance to break loose very often." Nnamdi responded, "I had a good time as well, it is always fun hanging out with you guys. But you are right though, Chi Chi, these long work hours put a grind on you. I know ya'll won't believe me, but sometimes I rather be back in law school looking over some case studies." Obi laughed and said, "Zik, you are on your own on that one. I feel you about working, but I don't even want to fathom doing law school over again. I don't know about ya'll, but those long hours of studying killed a lot of my brain cells and took a couple years off of my life." Nkechi said, "Yeah it is funny how time passes us by so quickly. I always remember all the fun times the three of us had together at Howard. We used to joke around about how we would start our own law firm together after a couple years of working. Now I am close to getting out of the legal field all together. It is crazy how life throws all types of twists and turns at you."

Even though Nkechi had told Obi and Zik about her plans the day before; Obi hadn't pressed her on the matter too much. Obi said, "We always talked about how Thurgood Marshall used the power of the law to push for equality of black people in this country. Although, the times have changed; the legal system will still play a huge role for the further progress for black people." Nkechi said, "I just don't believe whole heartedly in that line of thinking any more. I feel that black people have been bamboozled about the idea of integration. In theory it sounds like a good idea, black people move to white neighborhoods to get a better quality of life. But the reality is that after almost 40 years later, integration has only helped a selective percentage of black people, while the masses still have yet to experience anything." Nnamdi jumped in and said, "Chi Chi, I think you still might be drunk from last night. Are you trying to say that black people would be better off if segregation was still the law of the land?"

Nkechi said, "Zik, I never said nor do I believe such a thing. The problem is that we have to distinguish between civil rights and equal rights. Many people feel that the both of them are mutually inclusive, when in actually they are not. When people have been given civil rights, that implies that you have to treat them adequately, but you don't have to be fair or respectful to them. In the case of equal rights; it is something that has already been given to you at birth and you don't have to fight for it. We don't have to look any further than to our educational system. This year in May will mark the 55th anniversary of the United States Supreme Court overturning separate but equal in our schools. But sadly, today, 80 to 90 percent of black students are still stuck in low quality schools with the national dropout rate for us at 50percent, and even higher numbers in some communities."

Nnamdi said, "Chi Chi, the points that you have made are well taken and I agree with you. But in regards to the school, situation you know that everything boils down to where you live. If you live in a community with a lot of economic mobility, you pay more property taxes and if you live in the hood your property taxes are low. So since schools are funded by these property taxes, that is where the discrepancies lie." Nkechi said, "That is a great point and I was going to come back to that matter. That in my opinion is the elephant in the room that nobody discusses or just conveniently fails to bring up. In this country our schools are funded by a system that is structurally set up to favor predominantly middle class white kids over poor black and Hispanic kids. We all talk about how this area is the suburbs and another area is the ghetto. But isn't it true that all land is the same in nature. The thing that separates everything is by what is on top of the land and who assesses the value of that property. If we had Jim Crow laws in this country since the end of slavery, don't you think that in some way that would have negative effects on the economy of black people? Many of us don't understand that black people were literally shut out of the American economic system until the mid 1960s. So explain to me how black neighborhoods are supposed to have high quality schools when they don't have the tax base because there has never been any economic development what so ever in their communities."

Nnamdi didn't have any type of response for her after she made her statement. Obi said, "I don't think we have to say who won this debate between the both of you guys." Nkechi said, "Obi, this isn't about winning or losing anything. It is about making each other more knowledgeable about certain situations in our society. That is why I really want to work in these communities and help develop policies which we can demand the politicians to address. I know it won't be easy, but I feel that is the right thing for me to do at this moment in my life." Nnamdi said to her , "So I take it you aren't holding your breath about Obama really addressing the structural inequalities that you feel is affecting the country?"

Nkechi said, "I have a deep admiration and love for our African brother, but I don't think his administration will do too much to change anything. Maybe it's me, but I am not too caught up in this notion that he will be ushering in some new political era in America. In my opinion, he has been vague at best about what issues that he will be fighting for. I think that this recession will not allow him to be as ambitious as he wanted to be about his policies. But even though there is hope for Obama, I feel that the American public is really angry about this $787 billion dollar bailout the government gave to the banks to keep the financial system from collapsing. They feel that their government has sided with the rich guys instead of being in the corner for the average person. It is ironic that while the unemployment rate for black and Hispanic people has been ridiculously high for years, there was never a push to try and do anything about it, but now that the white middle class is feeling some pain, the politicians are moving heaven and earth to try and get things from getting even worse."

Obi shook his head in agreement with Nkechi's analysis and said, "Yeah it is funny how America says they are a capitalist country, but don't have any problem with practicing socialism in regards to protecting these large corporations. If it were up to me I wouldn't have provided those banks with a damn dime. These banks that created the whole home mortgage meltdown have been doing unfair lending practices in minority communities for decades. They would redline minority zip codes and either refused to offer them loans or just gave higher interest rates to the buyers even if they had good credit. I want to know what these black civil rights groups are going to do about this matter."

Nkechi responded, "If you ask me these civil rights groups' agenda has been misguided since the 1960s ended. They have become more geared in pushing diversity rather than equality along with being too intertwined with corporate America. You even see it when these civil rights groups raise the issue of questionable minority homeownership practices by these banks. These corporations will give millions of dollars to groups' general or scholarship funds and then that issue is over and done with just like that. So again nothing gets done but a promise that things will be better. I believe we have to push for a 21st century Black Nationalism, which involves black people controlling the economics and politics of their own communities. If these financial institutions are going to treat us like shit, we need to create our own banks that can meet the needs and demands for our people."

Nnamdi jumped in and said, "I see that you guys are the modern day Angela Davis and Huey P. Newton. It seems like ya'll are on some Karl Marx socialist type shit. I know that capitalism isn't great, but socialism is not any better; hell it would probably be worse." Nkechi responded, "Zik, your comparisons are very funny but I don't mind embracing them. I think we need to take another look at this capitalist system in the United States. A report that I read was released stating that the average CEO's of American companies' salaries and compensation I showed them making over 350 times the amount of the average worker. That figure is the highest discrepancy of any country in the world by a long shot. Some of these CEO's of these large financial institutions that went belly-up got multimillion dollar golden parachute packages, while their workers lost their income and healthcare benefits. You also see that the top 10 percent in this country control 90 percent of the all wealth as well. Also if you look how the wages for the average worker have been stagnant for the last 10 years; everything from food, healthcare, and energy prices have been rising at very high rates. Many people feel like things are getting out of hand in terms of them trying to keep up with their bills. So, if this is what you say is the best capitalism has to offer: I for one am open to whatever economic system will bring more fairness to the average person in this country. If you want to call it socialism or starting cooperatives, then so be it. I am not caught up in labels and things like that."

Nnamdi said, "Even though I don't always agree with your points, the both of you always make very strong intellectual arguments. I would like to continue our conversation, but right now I am hungry as hell and am in the mood for some Caribbean food," Nkechi said, "Yeah we can do that, there is a place that is right down the street from here." As the three of them made the short drive to the restaurant, Obi began to think about the long conversation that they had engaged in at Nkechi's place. If there was one thing that he missed the most was the intense debates that would go on.. As much as he thought he was well versed about issues, Obi would see how Nnmandi and Nkechi would always raise the level of the discussions. Also you couldn't come just saying any old thing, because you would get called out for not possessing any knowledge of what you were talking about. Once they got to the restaurant, they went to the first available booth to sit down.

Nkechi went to the bathroom not too much longer after they had arrived. Nnamdi said, "So what did you think about the conversation we had earlier? I always forget how hard Chi Chi is regarding things she is passionate about." Obi said, "Yeah that's how she has always been. She will always keep you are on your toes." Nnamdi looked at Obi with a big smile on his face. Obi looked at him and asked, "Why do you have such a big grin on your face man?" Nnamdi said, "I don't have any reason, just seeing you and Nkechi talk was interesting. It was like you guys are so much in sync with one another. I know we talked about the whole soul mate thing last night, but between the both of ya'll dancing last night and the conversation today just confirmed that she is the one for you." Obi asked, "Zik so how can you make a conclusion off of those things? I think we are very compatible, but I'm not sure about the whole idea that we are kindred souls or something." Nnamdi said, "It wasn't just me that made that assessment. After we had dropped y'all off last night, Ogechi mentioned the effortless chemistry between the both of you guys. So have you thought about your strategy about how you will try and come at Nkechi?"

Obi said, "I was thinking about that this morning after breakfast. It seems with everything going on I will just try and do it before the inauguration on Tuesday." While the both of them were still talking, Nkechi had gotten back from the bathroom. Shortly after that, they all put their orders in for their food. Obi asked, "So what are the plans for this evening?" Nkechi said, "Well I talked to one of my home girl's and she has some tickets for a concert tonight which will feature The Fugees." Nnamdi said, "Damn that will be a hot show on the real. I can't believe Lauryn Hill will actually be performing with Wyclef and

Pras. I know the group broke up and tried to come back but it didn't work out. I guess that Obama is bringing everybody together for this occasion." Obi said, "Yeah it will good to hear some real music for a change. Most of these artists now be rapping about nothing on their songs. The only thing they have is good beats but that is about it. ."

Nkechi said, "I think it is a mixture of us getting older and the hip hop-rap music has become too mainstream and pop. Let's be honest, when is that last time that you bought an album and second how many songs were actually jamming besides the singles? I just listen to my 90s R&B and hip hop and to jazz music." Nnamdi said, "Yeah you ain't never lied about the music game. I guess when we were younger we were spoiled by Tupac, Biggie, Jay Z and others just going hard all the time. It feels like we were growing up during the height of true hip hop and rap music in the 90s."

Obi asked, "So Chi Chi how is the going out scene in D.C.? I know it is wired up for the inauguration, but how is it on a regular weekend?" Nkechi said, "It is cool; I guess that I am older now and the whole club scene is just played out to me now. But right now everybody is on this whole urban professional thing. ." Nnamdi said, "What does the whole thing consist of." Nkechi said, "Well it is young black people who have graduated college and feel like they have some status. They are promoting a new sense of being grown which consists of going to wine tastings and eating exquisite foods like sushi." Obi started laughing and said, "That sounds like the same movement that is going on in Houston as well. It is funny going to these events, everybody comes looking fly and acting like they big shit or something. But it usually involves people drinking and just looking at each other trying to be cool. These are supposed to be networking mixers, but mostly everyone is there to be seen and not heard from."

Nnamdi said, "Damn that sounds like some straight up bourgeoisie type shit." Obi said, "Yeah Zik that is how it usually goes. I remember trying to strike up a conversation with a woman at one of these events. When we were going to exchange numbers, she asked me for my business card. I looked at her and said that I didn't have any on me at the time. She said when I get some to holla at her another time." Nnamdi was shaking his head and said, "I guess these are the times that we are living in now. I know that this Obama era will even make these urban professional events more prominent. There will be a lot more people wanting to go to these events to see if they can find their own Barack or Michelle." Nkechi said, "It sounds like we as black people are doing what we do best, just capitalizing on the moment. I would bet you that most of these people don't know anything about any of Obama's policies and won't try to be concerned even when he gets into office. I think a lot of black people just like the sense of power that Obama will be possessing."

Obi said, "I feel that everybody has this romanticized idea of what an Obama presidency will represent for the short and long term for this country. The media is pushing this notion of Obama taking us into a new post racial society in the United States." Nkechi said, "That is the new way of saying that everybody should assimilate and accept the mainstream culture which is seen out of a Eurocentric point of view. Their utopia would be to create a new race of dark skinned white people. I can only speak for me, but I am proud to be a Naija woman and wouldn't want it any other way. I love my dark skin, natural hair, and full lips so very much. I am of the belief that God made everyone on this planet to look different for a reason. He never intended for one group of people to be better than another based on physical features. Unfortunately, the Europeans have set the standard for beauty in this world and all the other cultures have followed them sheepishly. But I feel that the post racial thing goes deeper than culture with me. I feel that if we are truly post racial the legitimate grievances that blacks, Hispanics, and Native Americans will become part of the national conversation."

Obi jumped in and said, "All we have to do is look at what happened after Hurricane Katrina in New Orleans. It seemed that the media treated it like a black tragedy instead of an American one. I think that most white people don't feel that the inner cities of this country are actually part of America. You can even look at the strategy of how Obama side stepped the whole race issue during the campaign. Whenever he seemed like he was sympathizing with black people, his poll numbers with white voters went down. But when he was pushing that personal responsibility crap to us, his numbers went up with the same white voters."

Nkechi said, "You can also look at who he picked to be in his cabinet, beyond a few positions he gave to minorities and women. He went with the same standard white Ivy League educated men like all other previous administrations." Nnamdi said, "Chi Chi, I think you are being too harsh on Obama for his picks. He selected the best people based on experience and skill, not on race or gender." Nkechi responded, "So you are telling me there isn't a smart black man or woman or vice versa a Hispanic man or woman who could have been one of his economic advisers. Both groups make up 30percent of the population and should have some representation as they will be catching the most hell while this recession continues."

Nnamdi said to Obi and Nkechi, "I think you are expecting Obama to do more than he can. He is just the president of the country. He can't change the social structure overnight like you and others want him to do. All he can do is play within the boundaries and try to make incremental changes when the opportunity presents itself for him to."

Nkechi said, "I'm not looking for Obama to be a miracle worker or something like that. But I feel that his background along with his work as a community organizer allows him to be able to articulate the concerns of the various disadvantaged groups in the country unlike any other president in the history of the U.S."

The waitress finally brought their food and then the conversation ceased as they began to eat. Obi said, "Damn this Caribbean jerk chicken tastes good as hell. I have to take my time to enjoy it. After Nigerian food, Caribbean people are the only ones who come close to replicating our style of cooking." Nnamdi said, "They keep their food spicy just the way I like it." Nkechi said, "The both of you guys are real Naija men to the core. I can't see either of you marrying an akata woman, unless she is one who is willing to embrace our culture." Nnamdi asked her , "So would you date and marry a black American man." Nkechi responded, "I don't think that I would do so. It isn't because I am not attracted to black American men. But the reason for me is that I don't want to give up my Nigerian last name for an American one and I also would like my children to have Nigerian first and last names as well."

Obi said, "Chi Chi you are a Naija woman original. They don't construct too many women like you anymore. So do some of your black American women friends think that you are dissing on black American men." Nkechi said, "They know that I feel very strong about maintaining my culture so they don't say too much to me about it. Some of them actually want me to introduce them to some Nigerian guys to meet and get a change from dating black men." Nnamdi said jokingly, "Chi Chi you have got me thinking about starting a dating service for single black women who can't find a good black man. We can set these women up with eligible African men in this country and then maybe we could take this idea global. I see big dollar signs with this." Obi laughed and said, "Zik you are a fool for real. You know a lot of Africans will do it so they can try and stay or come into this country to get a green card." Nnamdi responded, "Obi you have made a good evaluation. We can put a disclaimer to let them know that results will vary case by case."

Nkechi was shaking her head in disbelief and said, "For an engineer and lawyer; Zik you say some dumb ass shit." Nnamdi said, "Chi Chi, don't be mad because I came up with the idea first. I am just applying the economic concept of supply and demand. I really want to help my black American sistas by hooking them up with a good man. Regardless, everyone is profiting off of this so called crisis for black women by writing books advising them who they should date, I just want to get my own little slice of the pie like everyone else is doing."

Obi said, "Well on that note, I am full and ready to head back to Nkechi's place and lay it down before we hit this concert up tonight." Nnamdi drove Nkechi and Obi back to her place and then left so he could head to Ogechi's place to get ready for the evening. As soon as they entered the apartment, Nkechi and Obi went straight to the living room to get some relaxation. Nkechi said, "I am happy to be back home, I was about to fall asleep at that restaurant. Obi responded, "I am with you on that one."

After a five-minute pause in the conversation, Nkechi asked Obi a question. "So tell me about how it goes down in H-Town?"

Obi answered, "What is it that you want to know about it?" Nkechi responded, "I have never been there before, so just tell me the basic stuff about the city." Obi laughed and said, "I will do my best to give some background information for you. Houston is the fourth largest city in the U.S.; the weather is pretty warm all year around, except in July and August, when the heat and humidity is unreal. The city is pretty laid back and not as fast paced as D.C. Finally, Houston is referred to as Little Nigeria. You can't go too far out here without seeing or hearing a Nigerian. I remember someone telling me that there is between 100,000 to 150,000 Nigerians in the city and that it has the highest population of Nigerians in the United States."

Nkechi said, "Damn, I know our people are running things out there." Obi agreed and said, "Yeah you already know how we do it. We Nigerians don't like to work for anybody for too long. We gotta run and control our own businesses. So when do you plan on coming out there to visit?" Nkechi said," Probably in the next couple of months or so. I have applied to your alma mater, University of Houston and along with Texas Southern as some of the schools that I am considering for my master's degree. I have also contacted some urban development organizations out there inquiring about some job opportunities. I am just trying to get the ball rolling, because I would like to start graduate school this fall."

Obi responded, "Well I see that you are on your grind the way you always are. Just let me know when you are coming, you know my door is always open to you." Nkechi said, "Thanks for the hospitality, I will give you plenty of advanced notice before I go out there. I don't want to interrupt anything with any jump offs that might be staying at your place." Obi laughed off the comment from Nkechi and said, "Chi Chi, you are like family to me, you don't have to worry about that. I already told you yesterday, that I don't have any women that I am messing with right now." Nkechi said, "I have heard that same line before, the next thing I know some woman is banging on your door saying that I am fucking with her man." Obi said, "Chi Chi you watch too much of these day time talk shows with those over the top storylines. I also forgot to mention that I only have a one bedroom apartment." Nkechi said, "That is not a problem at all, I guess you will be sleeping on your sofa." Obi looked stunned and said, "Well we will have to revisit that issue when you come out there."

Nkechi looked at her watch and said, "Damn, it is already 7p.m. we gotta start getting ready to hit up this concert. The line to get in will be worse than what we encountered last night at that other spot." Both Obi and Nkechi showered up and were ready to go within an hour. During that time, Obi began to see that Nkechi was pushing the envelope more than he would have thought. It was one thing for her to visit Houston, but for her to be actually applying to schools and jobs was a sign that she was aggressively looking for a long term relationship, which could lead to marriage. He had gotten the impression that their relationship would take on a gradual process, but it seemed things would be moving at a faster pace then he thought.

Obi would bounce the question off of Nnamdi when he saw him later this evening. The concert was located close to where Ogechi lived, so Nkechi and Obi drove over to her place to meet up with her and Nnamdi. Once they got to her place, Nnamdi and Ogechi were already in the car ready to go. Nkechi and Obi parked their car and jumped into Nnamdi's car. Nnamdi yelled as they entered the car, "So I see everybody is ready for round two tonight." Ogechi asked Nkechi, "So Chi Chi have you recovered from last night?" Nkechi responded, "Yeah girl, I'm doing well. I told these guys earlier today that I was just releasing some much needed stress and went a little bit overboard." Ogechi said, "I am happy to hear that you are fine, because you were pretty messed up when we left the club last night." Nnamdi said sarcastically, "Chi Chi was okay; she had her buddy Obi to nurse her back to full strength." Obi said, "Ogechi, I know you are not with this guy for his humor, because his jokes are lame and always miss the mark." Nnamdi laughed and said, "Don't be mad at me because I am telling the truth."

It seemed that everyone in the car knew something was brewing between Obi and Nkechi, but everyone was trying not to directly acknowledge what was going on. The four of them made a short 10 minute drive to the site of the concert. Once they parked the car, the four of them started to approach the entrance of the club. Nkechi's prediction of the crowd size was spot on as they saw a wave of people hanging outside of the club. Nnamdi said, "Damn this spot is off the da chain for real. I am happy we got our tickets and arrived here early."

Since they had pre sale tickets, the line to get in was only about 20 minutes compared to the longer wait time for those people trying to get in with no ticket. Once they got in, the four of them headed straight to the bar to buy some drinks. As Nnamdi was talking to the bartender he shouted out to him, "Okay, I need three crown and cokes and one glass of water with ice." Nnamdi started to stare at Nkechi with a smile on his face. Nkechi smiled and said, "Fuck you, Zik; you are always play around too much." Nnamdi said, "Chi Chi I always do things to get a reaction from you and it works every time." Nnamdi later told the bartender to make a fourth crown and coke.

They all made a toast to have a fun and safe night from

themselves. After about five minutes, Nkechi and Ogechi headed to the bathroom together. Once they left, Obi said, "It's wired up tonight in here, this concert should be good." Nnamdi said, "Yeah, The Fugees are always going to bring out a different crowd which consists of true hip hop heads and people on that Afrocentric vibe. It is a grown relaxed atmosphere with everyone just trying to listen and enjoy some good music." Obi said, "It is funny how we are enjoying this time hanging out with one another carrying on like we are in law school again and then after the inauguration things go back to normal. Sometimes I wish I could freeze time and keep all of us in one place." Nnamdi laughed and said, "That would be great if we could, but time doesn't stop for no one. We just have to cherish the moments that we get to spend with our family and close friends."

Obi said, "Zik you are right about that. I think I'm starting to feel a little nervous about turning 30. I can't say that I'm not envious of Chi Chi just to make the decision to quit her job and go into another direction with her career. It isn't that I don't enjoy working at my uncle's law firm, but it doesn't fulfill me anymore. Honestly, beyond graduating college and law school I don't feel like I have any real accomplishments in my life. I guess I always thought I would be further along in finding my purpose."

Nnamdi said, "Obi I think you are too hard on yourself. I think sometimes too many of us young people have these bloated views of how corporate America really is. Every new graduate that receives their bachelor's degree feels that when they get their first job out of college, that somehow they will be running the company by the time they reach the age of 30. We all know that climbing that ladder to the top involves other factors outside of just your work performance. In your case, unless you are going to die tomorrow I feel you have a long time to get to where you want to. I feel that our society dangles turning 30 like you are supposed to have your career and personal life all situated. Just look at Obama, he became the president of the U.S. at the age of 47. But it wasn't until he was 43, did he become a U.S. Senator after being a state representative in Illinois for many years with a few political setbacks along the way. In many people's eyes getting your dream job at 43 seems like you are off pace, but I am always reminded by something my parents always said to me; "Everybody doesn't go to sleep or rise from sleep at the same time." So just remember we will all reach our places in this world at different points and times from one another. I personally think you are on the right track."

Obi said, "Thanks for the words of encouragement Zik; I will take your advice on that matter." Obi asked Nnamdi, "So are you happy with where you are right now in your life?" Nnamdi, had a long pause and then said, "I can say that I am content with things at the moment. I have a well paying job, live in a nice townhouse, and am healthy. I guess you can say that I am just living life and enjoying being 32-years-old. I know that in the next few years I will probably reflect on my life and do some reassessing of my priorities."

As their conversation ended, Ogechi and Nkechi returned from the restroom. Nkechi said, "We need to move closer to the stage so we can get a better view of the performances." The four of them proceeded to walk to the center of the dance of floor. As the crowd started building up, the DJ played music to get everyone hyped up.. After 30 minutes, the DJ announced that The Fugees would be coming on. The crowd went crazy as the group came out. Everyone was singing along in unison as the group was performing their songs. After finishing up a few their songs, Wyclef and Pras left the stage for Lauryn Hill.

The crowd was waiting in anticipation of what she was going to do next. Finally she started singing her classic song, 'Turn Your Lights Down Low', which was made as collaboration with the late legendary reggae musician Bob Marley. The crowd again was even more hyped than they were previously. Nkechi was very gleeful about hearing the song. She said to Obi, "You know that this song is my jam." She started to grind on Obi as the performance continued. Nkechi was a huge Lauryn Hill fan; she always had a very emotional connection to her music.

While Nnmadi and Ogechi had went to the bar to get some more drinks, Nkechi was starting to feel tipsy and had gotten more physical with Obi in dancing and was now licking on his ears. She whispered into his ear, "I am horny as hell and I want to have sex with you later on tonight." Obi was taken a back a little bit by Nkechi's bluntness and responded to her, "Are you sure that you wanna take it there." Nkechi said, "Yes, I do. I have been repressing myself since you got here about doing it." Obi said, "So you aren't concerned about this being some type of one night stand." Nkechi laughed at the notion and said, "Well you are staying with me so that couldn't possibly happen and I know you want to do it with me as well." Obi asked, "Ok, do you wanna wait until the concert is over?" Nkechi said, "Any other night I would go, but Lauryn is jamming and I want to hear her sing her other songs." So they stayed until Lauryn Hill had finished singing her other songs.

After her performance ended, the club started to thin out and Nnamdi and Ogechi had come back to meet up with Nkechi and Obi. Nkechi said, "Where have you guys been? I didn't see the both of you during the whole show." Nnamdi looked and Ogechi and then smiled and said, "Well all I can say is that you guys aren't the only ones that were getting your freak on." Ogechi playfully hit Nnamdi on the arm after he said that comment. Nnamdi said to her, "Why did you do that? I was only telling them the truth. Anyway me and Ogechi were thinking about grabbing something to eat after we leave here, did you guys want to join us?" Obi said, "I am pretty tired man. I think that I am going to call it a night." Nkechi said, "I also feel the same way as Obi does. ."

As the four of them were walking towards the exit and to Nnamdi's car, Nkechi and Obi had started to feel on each other. The sexual tension between the both of them was very high, but they were trying to conceal it until they could at least get dropped off back at Nkechi's car. As soon as they entered her car, Obi and Nkechi started kissing all over each other. This continued while they were driving back to Nkechi's place. Once they got into the house, they were taking off each other's clothes very quickly. Obi was about to grab a condom when Nkechi asked him, "Do you just want to fuck me or do you want to have a relationship with me?"

Obi felt very perplexed at hearing Nkechi ask the question. He had wanted to have this conversation with Nkechi, but he didn't think it would be happening while he was literally minutes away from having sex with her. He said to her, "Maybe we should talk about this after we have finished doing what we were going to do." Nkechi starting pulling the bed sheets over herself to cover up her body. Obi knew that signified that her mood had shifted and he put the down the condom.

Nkechi asked, "So where are we going after you head back to Houston next week?" Obi said, "I know you said you were going to be coming down there in a couple of months to visit. I was thinking we could discuss the matter at that time." Nkechi said, "Well I think we need to establish what we are doing before that time happens. I know that I messed up in handling our situation when were finishing law school. But I made a vow to myself that I would do whatever it took to make it work again if the opportunity presented itself in the future."

Obi said, "Well I want to make it work between us as well. I was hesitant to attempt to push the issue between us in the past because I wasn't sure what you wanted. But now I see that you really wanna make this thing work between the both of us." Nkechi leaned over across the bed and gave him a big kiss on the lips. Obi started kissing on her and laying her down on the bed. Nkechi said, "What are you trying to do Obi." Obi said, "I thought since we figured everything out, we could get back to where we had left off at." Nkechi laughed and said, "No honey, we won't be doing anything tonight. Since we will be dating I'm implementing a three month policy on having sex." Obi said, "Chi Chi, I don't think we have to do that, we already know each other very well and I am not sure what the point of this rule is." Nkechi said, "Yes you are right Obi. But we know each other as friends, but not as lovers. The dynamics of our relationship will be changing so you have to get to know all facets of me and I will be doing the same with you."

Obi snickered and said, "I see that you have been getting your dating advice from Joan Clayton from the TV show, 'Girlfriends'." Nkechi laughed and said, "Yeah I could be doing that. Anyway are you okay with the arrangement." Obi said, "Well it's not the way I would ideally want it, but if this will make our relationship stronger than I am cool with it." After they finished the conversation, Obi tried to get in the bed and sleep next to Nkechi. She asked, "Obi, what are you doing?" He responded, "I am trying to go to sleep." Nkechi said, "I don't think that will be a good idea, there is too much temptation and I don't think either of us needs to be tempted to try and do something." Obi said, "Chi Chi, are you for real about this." She responded, "Yes I am Obi, I am sorry about doing this to you."

Obi sighed as he headed back to his bedroom. Nkechi said, "Okay babe, have a good night sleep and I will see you in the morning." Obi said the same greeting back to her as well in a grunting voice. As Obi was lying down in his bed, he had a hard time going to sleep as he had a serious case of blue balls from all the sexual anticipation of the night. But it also made him realize that he had to seriously do something about his situation with Tamika before Nkechi would be out there to visit him.

CHAPTER SIX

After a pretty chill Sunday which consisted of watching some NFL playoff games, Obi and everyone else in the world finally were ready for Monday to arrive which now made it officially one day till the inauguration and even more importantly was the national holiday of Dr. Martin Luther King, Jr. The holiday has always been known to be a day for people to do service in their community and not just a day off of work or school. This year's celebration was even more special with the ascension of Obama to the presidency only hours away. Obi and Nkechi had signed up to do some volunteer work in the community surrounding Howard University in the morning. While they were driving to their destination, Nkechi and Obi were discussing the MLK holiday.

Obi said, "It seems like everybody is trying to be involved in something today. I have never seen this level of attention for MLK's birthday on a national scale; mostly it is just celebrated by black people." Nkechi responded, "That is how it is most of the time. The media usually just interviews some old civil rights activists and asks them what Dr. King would think about America at this time. You would also see the president of the U.S. going to a black church and say how they were inspired by Dr. King and how their administration would push for policies to honor his legacy.

Obi said, "I read a poll that showed black people said they are more hopeful about race relations and that Obama is the fulfillment of the legacy of Dr. King." Nkechi said, "Black people are the most easily swayed people in the world. So now that America has one black president out of forty four they believe shit will be better. It is crazy how every black person when asked who they admire always say Martin Luther King Jr. We rarely acknowledge or embrace other figures like Malcolm X, Marcus Garvey, and the Black Panthers. It seems that we are scared of the reaction that white people will have to us saying that. The media and history has portrayed them as anti-American, radical militants when that is far from the truth. I feel for too long that everybody has given Dr. King this Disney like character image that minimizes the real impact and significance of his causes. The only thing that we are taught in school is that he believed in non violence, gave his 'I Have A Dream' speech in 1963, and then was shot dead in 1968."

Nkechi said, "In my opinion I think that the 'Beyond Vietnam' speech he gave exactly one year to the day before he died was his most important and realistic. Dr King voiced his opposition to the war in Vietnam and was concerned about how the escalation of the war would take away money from social programs in this country. I think we can see parallels today in how this country spends close to $600 billion a year on the military and defense in the budget, which is more than the top 20 industrialized nations in the world combined. That amount   doesn't include the billions of dollars to fight the wars in Iraq and Afghanistan." Obi said, "That connection you made is very spot on, but what stood out to me was how Dr. King said the country was moving from a person based society to a thing based one, where everything was measured on profit margins. That notion stems from King's acceptance of democratic socialism.

Before he died, he started to assess that the main problem facing black Americans was economic and that the capitalist system was not the answer for them or other poor people of different races in this country. It is interesting, that Dr. King's ideology had moved closer to Malcolm X's position even though they had different styles and tones in how they addressed racial matters." Nkechi said, "Most people don't know that when he died, Dr. King was one of the most hated men in this country. Black and white people together thought he was a traitor to his country for questioning President Johnson's stance in Vietnam especially after he fought and passed the substantive gains in bringing black Americans more into the American society. I don't think we would celebrate anything for King today if everyone knew his radical side."

After 30 minutes of driving, they reached their destination. As they met up with other volunteers and started working, Obi said to Nkechi, "It feels good to be back in the community trying to help out when you can." Nkechi said, "That is very true, so how much volunteer work have you been doing lately in Houston?" Obi said, "Honestly Chi Chi, until today, I haven't done anything in a few years. I guess that is one aspect from law school that I have fallen short on." Nkechi said, "Don't feel too bad about it that is how life happens sometimes, some priorities take the place of others." Obi said, "I feel that I want to make it more of a priority in my life. I have been brainstorming in what capacity I can help with certain community groups." Nkechi asked, "So what particular issue or issues do you feel strongly about that you would like to work on?" Obi looked baffled and said to her, "I guess I haven't thought about that matter too intently." Nkechi said, "You need to start identifying that first and then decide if you want to have your own organization or work on assisting with one."

Obi said, "Chi Chi it seems that you always have all the answers." He thanked her with a quick kiss on the cheek. The both of them were still adjusting to dating each other and the kiss took Nkechi by surprise. She at first was a little startled but then said with a smile, "No problem honey, the pleasure is all mine." After putting in about two hours of time work, the both of them left the volunteer site and headed back to Nkechi's place. They both were pretty tired and went to sleep upon their arrival. Since they would be waking up early the next morning to head to the inauguration at the Lincoln Memorial, they decided not to do any partying that night. Nnamdi and Ogechi would be coming over later to Nkechi's place for dinner and to just hang out and talk. Later on that evening, the four of them ate jollof rice, plantain, and black eyed beans that Nkechi had cooked. After eating, everyone went to the living room to relax. Nnamdi said, "Damn Chi Chi, I forgot how hard you be going in the kitchen. I am going to need to take some of that food to go." Nkechi said, "No problem Zik, I won't be able to finish all this food I made anyway." Ogechi said, "So is everyone ready for the big day tomorrow morning?" Obi said, "I definitely know I am. It seems like it's been forever since Election Day. It will be a moment that I think everyone will cherish forever." Nkechi said, "Yeah it will be cool, but then back to reality on Wednesday." Nnamdi said, "Dang, Chi Chi why do you have to be such a party pooper."

Nkechi responded with a laugh, "My bad for not singing kum bi ya like everyone else is doing. I guess I just am anxious to see what Obama will actually do instead of what people hope he will do." Obi said, "We all have debated about what limitations he will have to do things in this country, so I want to change gears for a minute. What are the prospects of Obama making a visit to Africa during his first term in office?" Everyone took a minute to digest the notion and then Nnamdi said, "It would be a great moment for our people all over the continent, but I think it will be a faint dream at best. I don't feel that Obama's advisers will allow it to happen. They had to battle all type of allegations about his citizenship during the election and going over there may heighten some conspiracy theorists even more."

Nkechi said, "I talked to my cousins in Nigeria and every one over there is excited about Obama. I think if he does go it will be a nice boost for the continent which has been displayed negatively by the Western media. He will embody some of the positives of the African people." Obi said, "I feel that there is more fear of what people think Obama will do in Africa than for black people in America. There is this notion by some people that Obama is a tribesman that has gained power which he will now share through friendly public policy and relaxed trade deals with various African countries." Nkechi said, "Hell that is what most Africans feel he should do. We already see that China is making big inroads in different countries in Africa by bringing them money for economic development in exchange for access to their natural resources. All of this is happening while America and the Europeans are still trying to keep the Africans at the kids table when it comes to being involved in global economics."

Nnamdi said, "This will be a very interesting four years not only in this country, but around the world as the Obama presidency takes shape." As the four of them continued talking for the next few hours it was close to 11 p.m. Nnamdi and Ogechi brought some clothes to spend the night at Nkechi's place. Obi began to think that this might provide a scenario for him and Nkechi to sleep in the same bed together. But all that went to the wayside when Ogechi and Nkechi decided to sleep in the same bed with one another. Nnamdi wasn't happy with the arrangements and said to Ogechi, "Why don't me and you sleep together." Ogechi said to him, "I am trying to get some sleep tonight; I don't wanna be up all night as you are trying to have sex with me." Obi didn't say much about the situation because he and Nkechi hadn't told Nnamdi and Ogechi about their new status.

The both of them figured it would be best to reveal everything a few weeks after things were a little more defined. Nnamdi went to sleep on the sofa after discussing his disapproval with Obi. Nkechi had set her alarm for 4:30 a.m. so that everyone could be up and hopefully ready to leave her place by 6 a.m. It was very cold in the early morning so everyone was pretty bundled up from head to toe. As they drove off on their way to the Lincoln Memorial, the streets were busy with everyone else going in the same direction. Nnamdi drove the four of them as close as could get and then they parked the car and then walked the final mile and a half to reach their destination. As they were walking, the streets were littered with people selling t-shirts of Barack Obama. After the very long walk, they finally reached the point they would be watching the inauguration from. As Obi looked around he saw the thousands of what was expected to be a million plus people descend on the Lincoln Memorial. The crowd consisted of people from every race, religion, and ethnicity across the globe. The inauguration wouldn't be starting until 12 p.m. and it was only 9 a.m. Nnamdi was getting restless.

Nnamdi said, "Damn it is cold as hell out here, if I knew it was going to be this bad I would have watched this shit at the house." Nkechi responded, "Zik stop complaining, you were the main one trying to be out here so you could witness history, right?" Nnamdi said, "Yeah, I did say it, but I didn't know this would be the price I would pay for it." For the remaining few hours everyone was just talking with one another and with other people who were waiting there as well. Obi watched on the big jumbo screens as the crowd had wrapped all over the Lincoln Memorial and beyond. As Nkechi saw him look at the crowd in awe she told him, "Everyone here needs to take a picture of this scene, because you will never see anything like this ever again in your lifetime." As great as the atmosphere was for the inauguration, when Obama finally got sworn in it happened so quickly you didn't get a chance to savor it.

After he gave his brilliant speech; the crowd dispersed as quickly as it had assembled. As they were walking back to the car, the four of them were pretty tired and too cold to discuss what just happened. They finally got to Nkechi's after fighting through traffic for an hour and half or so. As Obi and Nkechi exited the car, Nnamdi asked Obi, "So when are you heading back to Houston." Obi responded, "I will be heading out on Thursday morning." Nnamdi agreed and said he would call him later. Ogechi said, "Well Obi it has been a pleasure getting the opportunity to meet you and hang out. I talked to Zik and we will be planning to come to Houston so I will definitely see you again." Obi said, "That will be great; you guys just let me know. Take care of my boy. I know he is a hand full at times."

Obi and Nkechi went into the house and went straight to sleep. After they woke up, the both of them spent the rest of the day watching inaugural coverage on television. Nkechi had some tickets to a couple inaugural parties, but she and Obi decided to stay home and spend time with each other. The both of them wanted to relish the remaining day or so they had together before Obi would be heading back to Houston.

On Thursday morning, Nkechi and Obi woke up and prepared for his departure. It seemed that Nkechi had kept her emotions in check, but while they were driving she couldn't hold it in any more. Nkechi had a few tears in her eyes as she said to Obi, "I am really going to miss you so much, I wish we had more time to spend with each other." Obi said, "I know, but you will be down to see me in April for a week or so and we will be talking on the phone almost every day so it won't be too bad." For Obi it was a different to see Nkechi in this manner. He had never seen her cry or too emotional about much during their time in law school. he began to realize that he would be getting the girlfriend side of Nkechi that he never saw. After the long drive, they finally reached the airport. As Obi got out of the car to grab his luggage, Nkechi came out to help him. After that Obi gave Nkechi a big hug and they held on to each other for few minutes. They had a nice intimate kiss and said their goodbyes to each other. Once he grabbed his luggage and headed toward the baggage check in, Obi saw that Nkechi was still standing outside looking at him. Obi yelled to her in a smile, "Chi Chi, it is cold as hell out here, take your ass home and I will call you when I get back to Houston." Nkechi laughed and said okay and then entered her car and left.

Once Obi got onto the plane and got himself situated, his mind started drifting about his experience the last couple of days. He looked at his cell phone and saw the picture that Ogechi had taken of himself, Nnamdi, and Nkechi. Obi got a little emotional thinking about seeing the transition that he and Nkechi were going through. Once the plane was in the air, Obi's attention turned to the mountain of work that would be waiting for him.

Even though he was happy he went on the trip, he knew that everything you do has a price to pay in the end. He also started to think about how he would tackle the community advocacy he wanted to be a part of. Even though Nkechi told him he needed to be specific, he still hadn't nailed anything in particular down that he wanted to focus on. Also the Tamika issue was still not handled. It seemed with everything moving so quickly with Nkechi, that he hadn't thought of a way to end the situation with Tamika.

Obi knew that Tamika wasn't some chick he could just say that we are done fucking because I have someone else in my life. She was a woman that he had known and loved for over 10 years and in his opinion she deserved something more dignified than that. Obi started to get tired and slept for the rest of the trip back to Houston. Obi was awakened by the pilot saying that the plane was descending into Houston Intercontinental Airport. As Obi exited the plane, he was comforted by the warm temperature in Houston in contrast from the all the ice and brutal cold weather he left in D.C. He quickly got his luggage and his car; then headed to his apartment.

He sent a quick text message to Nkechi that he made it back safely and that he would call her later that evening. Obi went to sleep and took a three hour nap until he was awakened by a phone call. It was his Uncle Ugo and he wanted to know about the trip. "Obi, my boy how are things going with you, have you made it back to Houston." Ugo said. Obi was still getting himself together from sleep and said, "Yes, uncle I got home a few hours ago. I just got up from a quick nap." Ugo said, "That is good to hear. Well I know you enjoyed yourself and got the much needed relaxation and experience you were seeking from this trip." Obi said, "I got a lot out of this trip uncle. I will talk about it with you when I come into the office on Monday." Ugo said, "That will be okay, I need to talk with you about another matter as well."

It seemed that Ugo had opened up the gates because after his call Obi received calls from his mother and Chike. He spent the next few hours talking with them and never went back to sleep. Obi spent the next couple of days trying to recover and didn't do too much besides talk with Nkechi on the phone. As Obi went to work on Monday, he was asked by everyone in the office about how D.C. was and what he was doing out there. He spent much of the morning talking with Miss Washington and Miss Jackson about everything. It wasn't until after lunch that he was able to speak with his uncle. Obi was excited walking to Ugo's office so he could tell him about his situation with Nkechi, but he saw that his uncle had a very somber look on his face. Once he sat down he asked his Ugo "Is everything okay with uncle?" Ugo responded hesitantly, "Yes Obi I am fine." Ugo walked around the room and closed the door. Obi started to think to that his uncle was about to tell him some bad news. Ugo said, "Obi I don't know how to tell you this but I don't know how much longer I will be able to keep the law firm running."

Obi looked in shock and said, "Uncle, I know that you said that the finances were a little unsteady, but I had no idea things had reached dire straits." Ugo said, "Yes, my nephew I didn't want to cause too much alarm for you or the other workers. My health has not been too good either, I recently have been having chest pains and the doctor says that I need to start taking it easy." Obi had thought about telling Ugo that he could take over the law firm, but he had other things he wanted to pursue and wasn't ready to take on full duties of running a small business. Ugo had hoped that Obi would seize the opportunity that was presented to him, but he saw that his silence on the matter spoke louder than words. But he also knew that he had thrown a huge curve ball to Obi and that he needed to give him time to take everything in. Obi asked Ugo, "So when do you think that you plan on shutting everything down." Ugo responded, "It will probably be at the end of this year, I think that will be good enough time to close out open cases any also give everyone a chance to look for a new job." Obi asked his uncle if there were any other matters to discuss, Ugo said no and with that Obi thanked Ugo for his time and walked back to his office.

As Obi was sitting back in his office, he felt very dejected. This wasn't the news he wanted to hear after his trip to D.C. He started to think about where his next job would be at. It had been almost three years since Obi had to think about this situation. He didn't dwell too much on what his uncle had told him because there was still a lot of work to do at the office along with doing taxes for people. For the next two months, Obi worked long hours and rarely spoke to anyone besides t Nkechi on the phone. She was planning on coming to Houston at the end of April to see him, check out the city, and visit the schools that were on her list. Their relationship was going as well as any long distance could go. They would talk on the phone for a few hours a night and throw in a little phone sex to make it interesting. Obi also found out the hard way that in the end of the day that regardless of their friendship, Nkechi expected Obi to be more emotional and romantic with her like most women. The transition was taking some getting used to, but they were making it work.

Obi didn't tell Nkechi what was happening at the law firm. He thought that by saying so, that would make her reconsider her plans, since his work situation wasn't stable. Obi and Tamika were sending text messages, but because of his busy schedule they hadn't met up yet. Even though things with Nkechi were going great, he still had a yearning for some pussy. It was going on almost four months since he last got some and it was getting harder every day to hold out. He actually was happy he hadn't seen Tamika because he knew something would probably go down between the both of them.

Obi was barely keeping up with everything going on in the first couple months of the Obama presidency. He knew that the Democrats had passed a huge economic stimulus bill through Congress with a lot of criticisms and little support from the Republicans. The bill was supposed to give relief to local and state governments along with Americans struggling through the ongoing recession. There was also news that Obama would be taking a trip to the Middle East in June along with stops to possibly some African countries as well. The countries that he would be traveling to had yet to be disclosed. Obi was surprised that Obama would make that trip so early in his administration, but he was happy to see that he would be going out there. As he was reading the websites and blogs in Nigeria; it seemed like a foregone conclusion that Obama would definitely be coming there on his visit. Obi also thought he would go to South Africa to meet with Nelson Mandela, and finally Obama would touch down in his father's homeland of Kenya. Obi started to think that Obama would be more transformative than Nkechi was saying he wouldn't be. One day after work, Obi got an unexpected call from his father. Since he had gotten back home from D.C., the two of them talked sparingly but nothing too detailed. Obi father's said, "How is everything going on with you my son?" Obi responded, "Everything is going well, I am just getting home from work." His father said, "Oh okay, have you started to make any plans for yourself upon the pending closure of your uncle's business." Obi said, "Honestly father, with the all the work I have been doing I haven't had too much time to think about the whole matter." Chukwuemeka said, "I understand, it came as a bring shock to everyone. All I can say is that life moves on and I know you will put yourself at another good company. The main reason for my call though is that The Nigeria Club is seeking to induct some new members into the organization this fall. I wanted to know if you would like to join the group." Obi said, "Whoa, I don't know what to say right now on the matter. It seems that with everything going on I am not sure if I have the time or money to make a commitment to the organization right now."

Chukwuemeka laughed and said, "My son, you know I am the chairman so you don't have to worry too much about it. I will sponsor you and pledge the initial $1,000 needed to get the ball rolling for you." Obi said, "Well, father give me some more time to think about it and I will get back with you later on the matter." Chukwuemeka said, "That is fine, but don't wait too long to make a decision. You know this is a very prestigious and professional organization so a lot of people will be eager and ready to become a member. Anyway when will we be meeting this woman you are currently dating right now?" Obi had discussed with his mother about how everything was going on with Nkechi. His mother had met Nkechi when she visited Obi at Howard and always felt like she was a good fit for him. Obi said, "She will be here at the end of April for about a week." Chukwuemeka said, "Good, make sure we get to see her face now. I am happy you will be bringing home one of our beautiful smart Naija women. I know you were dating that one akata girl and she was a good woman, but only our women will know how to treat you very properly." Obi said, "Yes father, I will let you know and I will also tell her that you asked about her."

After that the two of them discussed some other issues and then the phone conversation ended. Obi began to think about his father's idea for him to join The Nigeria Club. Like his father said the organization was one of the high profile Nigerian's groups to be a part of. The group was an outlet for Nigerians to enjoy their culture and network amongst themselves. But beyond that the benefits consisted of helping members pay for the costs of a death of a family member in the U.S. as well as in Nigeria. They also had receptions for members who had kids who graduated high school or college along with attending the marriages of some of the members' kids. All in all it was a great group to be involved in. The problem though is that there is always a lot of infighting amongst the members for who will be leading the particular branch in that city. It would be funny and sad at the same time to see professional grown men and women fighting and cursing each other out like small kids. Obi didn't think that the group did anything to enhance or influence Nigerians who weren't a member of the club.

Most of the parties or events that were thrown consisted of people just patting themselves on the back and spraying dollars all over the place. Obi didn't particularly like the social class aspect of the group. He felt that everyone should be proud of their academic and professional accomplishments, but it was another thing to be a braggart and arrogant, as though you were more superior to those who didn't have your same status. Obi rarely heard anyone talk about giving college scholarships to low income Nigerian students in Houston or trying to determine what type of special projects to work on for those back in Nigeria. The sad part was that for all the hundreds of thousands of dollars that had been raised by the group; they didn't even have their own building where they held their events.

Obi also knew that he would be coming in as a new member and young guy, so any of his new ideas of doing things would probably be brushed off to the side. Since his father was leading the group, he didn't voice his displeasures with the way the organization was run; to avoid any arguments between them. But his uncle Ugo felt the same way that Obi did about the group. Ugo was a member for a few years, but quit the group after seeing that the meetings consisted of people just gossiping about the other members with no tangible items ever being discussed. Later on that evening, Obi got a call from Tamika. She said, "Hey Obi, are you at home right now." Obi said, "Yeah what is up." Tamika said, "Oh okay, I am right down the street from your place I was going to stop by if that was cool."

Obi didn't know if he wanted her to come by or not. He hesitated for about 30 seconds and reluctantly said, "Yeah that is fine, come on over." Once he hung up the phone with her, Obi started to panic about what might take place. He decided in his mind that nothing was going to happen between them so he would be cool. After about 10 minutes, Obi got a knock on his door and it was Tamika. She came in looking fine as hell as always. They embraced each other and she gave him a big kiss on the lips. Tamika said, "I have been waiting to do that for awhile now." Obi acted like he didn't want her to do it but he was lying to himself.

As they went to sit down on the couch, Obi asked her, "So what brings you over to my side of town at this time of the night." Tamika responded, "Nothing really, I haven't seen you in a couple months, just wanted to make sure everything was good with you. I was starting to think that you might be messing around with another woman or something." Obi felt a big gulp in his throat after she made that comment. Obi responded with a laugh and said, "I have just been really busy since I got back from the inauguration with work." Obi felt that this was probably a good time to tell Tamika about ending their sexual relationship. But just staring at her made him real horny and he started to feel that his urges would get the best of him. Once she excused herself to go the bathroom, Obi started to think what he was going to do. He knew he couldn't betray Nkechi and have sex with Tamika.

As he was trying to grasp all these thoughts in his head, Tamika had come out of the bathroom only wearing a thong with her double D tits sitting up plump and perfect. Obi knew that he was done for once that happened. As she approached him, she started kissing all over and then took off his pants and gave him head. In his heart, Obi knew that he was fucking up, but the shit felt so good. After a few minutes of that, Tamika asked Obi to get the condoms. Obi felt that this could be his chance not to have sex with her. Obi said, "I don't have any on me right now." As he was starting to put up his pants with, Tamika had went into her purse and pulled out a condom. She said, "I have one right here." Obi's face turned stone cold as he saw it in her hand. He knew that it was now or never if he was going to say anything.

As Tamika grabbed his hand and they headed to the bedroom, Obi stopped and said, "Wait Tamika I can't do this." She said, "What is the wrong with you." Obi sat down on the couch and said, "Tamika, I don't know what way to tell you this, but I am seeing someone right now." Tamika was taken aback by what that and said, "So how long has this been going on." Obi responded, "Actually it just started when

I went to D.C. My friend Nkechi and I kinda of started falling for each other while I was up there. We have been dating since I got back here." Tamika said, "So why didn't you tell me this whole time." Obi said, "I wanted to tell you, but it was hard for me to do it. It took me a while to come to grips with the idea of another woman being better than you. But I guess it took me going to D.C. to realize that the woman had been there for awhile." Tamika by now was sitting on the couch alongside Obi. She had realized that her worst nightmare had come to past. Obi had finally moved on to another woman. Tamika acted very resolute and said, "Well I don't have any one to blame but myself. I didn't treat you like the prized commodity that you are. I don't know if there is any way that we could make it work between us again."

Obi wanted to say yes in his heart, but in his mind he and Tamika weren't there anymore. He knew that for him to turn down having sex with Tamika without Nkechi finding out meant that he had moved beyond her. Obi said, "At this time Tamika I don't think that will be possible." Tamika didn't say a word as she went to the bathroom and got dressed. As she was about to head to the door, Obi looked at the clock and it was after midnight and it was raining pretty heavy outside. He said to her, "I don't think you should be on the roads, you can stay here if you want to."

Tamika looked back at Obi with a smile and accepted his offer. While they were sleeping on Obi's bed, Tamika was persistently trying to have sex with Obi. She was kissing all over his body and started giving him head again. Obi was trying to resist what she was doing, but he finally stopped fighting it and they had sex. After they finished having sex, Tamika felt empowered that she could still make Obi do what she wanted him to do. But in the end it would be little solace for her because Obi would no longer be waiting for her any more. Her emotions got the best of her as she sobbed herself to sleep.

CHAPTER SEUEN

Obi was excited that he was finally closing in on the end of his hectic work schedule as he was preparing the remaining tax returns for his clients. In his mind, April 15th couldn't have come fast enough. He was also happy as well because Nkechi would be coming down to visit at the end of the week. As Obi was doing some cleaning up at this place, he got a call from Chike. "What's been going on man, I haven't heard from you in awhile cousin. How is life been treating you." Chike said. Obi responded, "I have been doing well, just staying busy finishing up these tax returns. But I finished everything up last night, so I am a free man again." Chike said, "That is great to hear man, anyway me and Lamar was talking about going to The Chill Spot later this evening and seeing if you wanted to fall through for a bit." Obi said, "Hell yeah, I need a drink after all this shit I have been doing lately." Chike laughed and said, "Alright, man that is a bet. We will be up there at around 8 p.m."

As they hung up the phone, Obi was happy to go out and hang with Lamar and Chike. He had a lot to bring them up to speed on about everything with Nkechi and Tamika. Obi recently told Nnamdi about him and Nkechi, but that was after Nkechi slipped it out to him while they were talking on the phone. Nnamdi wasn't surprised at all and knew that something was going to happen between the both of them. After a couple of hours of doing more things around his place, Obi got ready and started heading out to The Chill Spot.

Once he arrived he saw that Lamar and Chike were already on the patio. Obi dabbed up Lamar and Chike as he entered the place. Lamar said, "Damn Obi, you have been M.I.A. since you got back from D.C." Obi said, "Yeah, man I was on the grand hustle since I got back." Obi and Lamar texted each other during that time, but it was just to say what's up and nothing more than that. Lamar responded, "So how was the inauguration, I know there were a lot of females out there." Obi said, "Yeah man I can't lie there was tons of beautiful women out there. But to be honest I didn't holla at any of them." Lamar said, "Why not man, that is what you were talking about before you left to go up there." Obi said, "Things kind of just happened while I was up there with my friend Nkechi and I started picking up our vibe we had in law school and decided to start dating." Chike said, "Wow that is good to hear Obi. So what are you guys going to do about the long distance thing?" Obi said, "Well she is quitting her job and moving out here to start graduate school in August. She will be out here this weekend to check out some schools and visit with me as well." Lamar said, "So what are you going to do about Tamika?"

Obi responded, "Actually she came by the spot two weeks ago and caught your boy at a weak spot and we ended up fucking."

Lamar laughed and said, "Obi I didn't know you had it in you to fuck over a woman." Obi said, "I didn't plan on doing nothing. I explained the situation to her and it was raining kind of bad that night and I told her to stay the night and then it happened." Chike said, "Obi, do you plan on telling Nkechi about what you did." Lamar jumped in and said, "Obi don't tell that your girl nothing man. You guys are starting a fresh relationship and this will only fuck it up."

Obi said, "I gotta go with what Lamar said, it wouldn't be in my best interest to say anything to Nkechi." Chike said, "You do what is best for you, anyway I am happy that you have finally got past dealing with Tamika. How did she take it when you told her the news?" Obi said, "She felt like she fucked up pretty much. But she didn't really say anything different that she would do to persuade me to stay beyond just sex." Lamar said, "The reason is she can't do anything more than that. Most women are pretty confident that having some good pussy a is enough to make a dude not go anywhere. But she knows she couldn't compete with a woman like your girl Nkechi who has all the right things to keep you happy beyond the sexual stuff." Obi said, "I never thought of it like that before, I guess I was just too caught up in the whole aura of Tamika."

Lamar asked, "So are you going to keep fucking Tamika until your girl moves down here permanently?" Obi gave Lamar a confused look and said, "Hell nah, man. I am trying to be committed to Nkechi and that won't happen if I keep messing around with Tamika." Lamar smiled and said, "Obi, you sound like a man already in love with Nkechi. I respect you for that, but you have to realize that once she moves down here you will be damn near married to her." Obi said, "Lamar, that is not going to happen. She will probably stay at my place until she can get on her feet and then find her own apartment." Lamar said, "That sounds good to say in theory. But I will bet everything I own that once she moves in with you that she ain't ever leaving. Once you get used to that in house pussy and having breakfast and dinner waiting for you, things will change my nigga."

Obi said, "So if that does happen, what is so wrong with that?" Lamar said, "There isn't anything wrong with that, but you might as well get as much side pussy as you can, because you won't be getting any new pussy for a long time or maybe ever once your girl Nkechi moves down here." Chike laughed and said, "Obi, don't listen to Lamar, this dude will never get married with the attitude he has about women." Lamar said, "I believe in marriage, but I am in my prime right now, I still got a few years in the game before I think about putting my playa jersey into the rafters. . Just thinking about settling down makes me feel uneasy."

Obi said, "I will be content with just having sex with Nkechi." Lamar said, "So have you guys had sex yet." Obi reluctantly said, "No we haven't done it yet. We were close when I went up there, but she wanted to have a three month rule before sex." Lamar and Chike started laughing at that notion. Lamar said, "Ok, now that is some funny ass shit. But real talk, what happens if the sex ain't as good as it is with Tamika." Obi said, "I guess we will find out, if it is off the chains than that is great for us. If it is not great, then the both of us will work on getting it there." Lamar said, "Obi you have always been an eternal optimist about everything." The three of them got some drinks and continued their conversation for another hour or so. Later, Lamar decided it was time for him to go home. Obi and Chike decided to stay out for a little longer to talk some more.

Chike hadn't talked to Obi about everything that was going on at his father's law firm. "So have you started the process of looking for another job yet, Obi?" Chike said. Obi responded, "I guess I have been putting it off with all the work I have been doing. But it seems that now I have to start making some tough decisions about my next move." Chike said, "So do you wanna go into the private sector or maybe get on with another law firm?" Obi said, "I have been thinking about those options, but regardless it won't be like working for your father."

Chike responded, "I know this is out of left field, but have you thought about taking over the law firm and running it yourself?" Obi said, "I did think about that when your father first told me the news, but that would mean that I would be working a lot more hours and basically have no life. I just am not up to that challenge right now." Chike shook his head and said, "Obi you are always talking about getting your chance to make a difference in the world. It seems like this is your golden opportunity and you are running away from it. If you take over the law firm you will have total control of everything." Obi responded, "Chike, it isn't as easy as you are saying. There is a big financial risk for me trying to do what you are suggesting. I also would need to hire at least one more experienced lawyer and still pay the remaining staff that we have employed." Chike said, "Obi I never said that it wouldn't a difficult task to undertake." Obi said, "So what do you think your father thinks I should do?" Chike said, "Obi you know my father isn't one to interject too much into what someone should do. He hasn't told me this, but I feel that he would like you to take over the firm. This is something he built by himself from the ground up and he would hate for all his hard work to come to abrupt end now."

Obi said, "Well I will take it into consideration and talk with your father in the next week or so." After that Obi and Chike left The Chill

Spot and headed home to their separate destinations. As Obi was driving home, he was thinking about the conversation that he and Chike had finished. He started to realize that he wasn't all too thrilled about going to work for someone else. Just hearing the stories of what Nnamdi and Nkechi were enduring didn't make him want to make the leap into corporate America. But he also knew that running the law firm went beyond just the financial aspect of things. During most of his time at the firm, Obi didn't deal with too much beyond just finishing up his work in a reasonable amount of time. He never had to handle any real managerial responsibilities like employee benefits, maintaining and getting new clients, and various other things that his uncle took care of.

Obi knew that he wouldn't be able to keep his carefree lifestyle that he currently was living right now. It was a lot for him to digest at the moment, but he decided not to worry about it at the present time. The next few days flew by up to the arrival of Nkechi. Even though the both of them gave themselves a lot of encouragement over the phone, it wasn't the same as having that person right in front of you. Obi went to the airport and picked her up on Friday afternoon and brought her back to his place. Once they got to Obi's place, Nkechi was commenting on how big and spread out Houston was. She said, "Damn, I thought we would never get to your place. This city is huge for real; it makes D.C. look like a small city. ."

Nkechi walked over to Obi and gave him a tight hug and kiss on the lips. Obi said, "What was all of that for." Nkechi responded, "It isn't about anything at all. I am just happy to see my man in the flesh." Obi said, "Well I am happy to see you as well. I think we will have an interesting and fun time this week coming up." Obi and Nkechi spent the rest of that night chilling and on Saturday the both of them went out to different places in the city. Like most women, Nkechi wanted to do some shopping. Nkechi and Obi decided they would go to the Galleria Mall to give Nkechi a wider variety of stores to choose from. As the two of them were walking all over the place; they both enjoyed each other's company immensely.

Obi was never a fan of holding hands or showing affection in public, but he did so, without thinking when he was with Nkechi. After a couple of hours, they left the mall and went back to Obi's place. Once they got home they ate some food and discussed the plans for Sunday. "Obi said, "My parents want to meet you tomorrow. So we will meet them at church and then go over to their house for dinner." Nkechi said, "That sounds like a chill Sunday to me. I have to admit that I haven't been to church in a couple of years though. At this point in my life, I am looking to have a more spiritual relationship with God which is not defined by a particular religious ideology. I am still a Christian, but I don't know about following every tenet of the bible so ridgedly. . But hearing and reading about what is happening in Nigeria between the Christians and Muslims gives me grave concerns. The continued violence and bloodshed in northern Nigeria is starting to become very unspeakable. We are killing ourselves over each other's religious beliefs.

Obi said, "I agree with you wholeheartedly about everything you said. Sometimes I wonder if the country needs to be split into two countries between the North and South." Nkechi laughed and said, "That is something that will never happen at all. Our parents' generation is still bitter about how the Yorubas didn't join with the Igbos to go against the Hausas in the Biafra-Nigerian War. Everybody knows the oil is in the south, which is predominately were the Igbos reside. Do you think that for one second that the Hausas will let their share of the oil revenue go?" Obi said, "The answer to your question is no; they will not. They would rather fight another war before that ever takes place. We Nigerians have to learn that we are stuck with each other. All our tribal and ethnic groups need to think about the best interest of the country, instead of their own petty needs. Nigeria will rise or fall collectively as one country. This topic is one that you can debate with different Nigerians and everybody has their own opinion. Well let us switch to something that is a little less complex. What do you want to get into tonight?" Nkechi said, "This is your city Obi, you are supposed to be telling me what is going down on a Saturday night." Obi said, "I know that this Nigerian lounge that be jumping late night if you want to do that." Nkechi said, "That sounds like a plan to me. I am in the mood to hear some Nigerian music anyway. So the both of them got ready and started to head out to their destination. They didn't arrive to the club until 12:30 am, but nevertheless the spot was already jumping.

Most Nigerian clubs stayed open until 4am, so Obi and Nkechi were getting there at its prime time. The music selection of the DJ consisted of old school Nigerian music, reggae, American hip hop and R&B. Obi and Nkechi were dancing hard from the time they entered the place. As they went to take a break from dancing, they both headed to the bar. The club was serving food as well so they both got some suya and meat pie. As the two of them were eating and drinking, the DJ announced he was playing some music from a new R&B duo from Nigeria called P-Square. The name of their song was 'No One Like You'. The both of them were heading to the dance floor as the song was playing. They really enjoyed the melody and lyrics of the song.

They were dancing face to face while playfully smiling at each other. Nkechi said, "This is one of the sweetest and most romantic songs I have ever heard in my life and for it to come from Nigerians makes it even better. Whenever I get married this will be my official wedding song for real." Obi smiled at Nkechi's comment and said, "So I hope that I get an invitation when you do get married." Nkechi sarcastically said, "You will definitely be there, but hopefully you won't be sitting in the pews." After the song ended, Obi looked at his watch and realized it was almost 3a.m. He told Nkechi it was probably a good time for them to leave so they could head home to get some sleep before church in the morning.

As they were driving back his place, Obi thought this might be the night for them to finally have sex. But Nkechi was already nodding off in the passenger's seat. Obi woke her up as they reached his place and the both of them went to his bed to lie down. Once they were in the bed, Obi whispered into Nkechi's ear if she was ready for something to go down. Nkechi was half way and said that they would do it at another time. Obi was a bit disappointed, but he was kind of tired himself and didn't push the matter too much. The next morning was a struggle for Obi and Nkechi to wake up for church. They sluggishly got ready and dressed and started heading out there. While in the car Nkechi asked Obi, "I hope that I make a good impression with your parents." Obi laughed and said, "Don't worry Chi Chi, you will be fine. Everybody will love you. My aunt and mom might quiz you on your cooking skills but that is about it." Nkechi said, "I know how our Nigerian mothers are concerned about their son's eating habits after they get with a woman besides them. I have two brothers and my mother does the same thing to all of their girlfriends too." Once they got to the church Obi and Nkechi saw his parents along with Uncle Ugo and Aunt Nkiru. Nkechi greeted Obi's family briefly before the church service began.

After the service, they congregated outside of the parking lot talking for awhile. Obi's mother said to Nkechi, "Ada, how are you doing this afternoon. I hope all is well with everyone in your family." Nkechi said, "Madam, thanks for your concern. We are all doing very well." The other family members had swarmed Nkechi to find out more about her. Obi said, "Before you guys give her the sixth degree in terms of questions, let us go to the house first." Everyone agreed and got into her vehicles and headed to Obi's parents house. Once they got there, Obi's mother and aunt headed to the kitchen to prepare Sunday dinner. Nkechi decided to follow them to help out as well. Obi, Ugo, and Chukwemeka had headed to the living room to sit and talk. While in the kitchen, Aunt Nkiru shouted out to Obi, "So how does Nkechi's cooking compare to mine and your mother's?"

Obi hesitated as he was trying to come up with a neutral answer. Ugo started laughing and said, "Obi you are in a no win situation on that one. The best thing to do is act like you didn't hear the question." Obi said, "Auntie, I didn't hear what you said clearly can you repeat it again." The three women came out of the kitchen and went into the living room and repeated their question again to Ugo. Obi's father saw how uncomfortable the situation was making him and said, "Ijeoma and Nkiru, Obi will always love your food forever, but he is a man now and his woman's meal will have to take precedence at this point."

As the two women griped a little bit, Nkechi blew Obi a kiss as she went back into the kitchen. Obi looked at his father and said, "Thanks father for getting me out of a very tight spot." Chukwuemeka said, "No problem my son. You must realize that mothers get jealous when their cooking isn't number one with her sons any more. It happens to every man as he comes closer to finding his wife." After another hour and half, the food was ready for everyone to eat. While they were eating at the table, Chukuemeka asked his wife, "So how did Nkechi hold her own in the kitchen with the veteran chefs." Obi's mother said, "She did an excellent job in my opinion. I know her mother has taught her very well." Obi in his mind was happy that his mother had given Nkechi her seal of approval in that regards. Ugo asked Nkechi, "So Obi tells us you will be moving down her to go to graduate school for Urban Policy." Nkechi responded, "Yes sir that is right. I have told Obi how unfulfilled that I have been with my present employer. The money they pay is good, but even that couldn't keep me there." Chukwuemeka said, "So you want to help the akatas with economic issues in their community. I think you might be wasting your time in my regards my dear."

Obi wanted to jump in and say something, but he saw that Nkechi was going to respond to his father's question. "Well in all due respect sir, I don't feel that it will be waste of my time. Everyone has been telling our generation to chase power and status in our professions. I have been doing that for the last couple years and I want to start going after the dreams that I wanted to pursue when I was in law school. I think too many Nigerian parents think the only way their kids are successful if they make a lot of money and have some titles in the front and back of their names. I feel that success is determined about what impact your work is having on other people. I know that finances are important, but in the end I don't want to be only defined by that narrow scope."

Everyone was silent at the table after Nkechi's comment. Obi felt that his parents wouldn't like how assertive she was with his father. After they finished talking some more, everyone started taking their plates to the kitchen. Ugo pulled Obi aside to talk with him very quickly. Ugo said with a smile, "You have a very strong willed woman on your hands. She doesn't take shit from anybody. I think you might have found yourself a winner Obi." Obi said, "What do you think that my father will say about it." Ugo said, "I think he will concur as well. If you haven't realized it already we Ifeanyi men always marry very nice and supportive women, who also can stand up to their men when need be. Every man needs a woman to help him clear out his eyes when he can't see properly at times. This type of woman will always have your best interest at heart at all times. She will give you a little hell here and there, but that is what all women will do at least one point or another in your marriage." Obi thanked his uncle for the words of wisdom. He still hadn't made a decision about the law firm and felt this wasn't the best time to take about it either.

The evening time had come and Obi and Nkechi started to head back to his place. Everyone gave a warm embrace to the both of them as they were leaving. Obi's mother had exchanged numbers with Nkechi. She also told Nkechi to have her mother call her so they could talk as well. Obi's mother looked at him and said, "I have Nkechi's number, so if any problems happen amongst you two I will try and patch work them as soon as possible." Obi laughed and said, "Okay mama, I don't think that you will have to worry about that for the time being.."

On the way home, Obi and Nkechi talked about the outing at his parents' house. "So do you think I came across a little too forward in the conversation with your father?" Nkechi asked. Obi said, "I think you were okay, sometimes he needs to take heed to some of the subjects that you brought up. Regardless, everyone seemed to like you a whole lot." When the both of them finally arrived at Obi's place, they watched television for the rest of the evening. During this time, Obi thought this would be a good opportunity to ask for Nkechi's opinion about his decision about the law firm. "Chi Chi, I have something that I wanted to ask you." Nkechi turned the volume down on the television and said, "What is it honey." Obi said, "Well I haven't mentioned it to you, but my uncle's health is not good and it won't allow him to continue running the law firm after this year. He hasn't come out and asked, but my cousin said he thinks my uncle wants me to take over the business. Nkechi gave him a big hug and said, "That sounds like wonderful news, Obi. So I know you are excited about everything." Obi said, "Well I haven't really decided on what I am going to do right now." Nkechi said, "So what is holding you back from making a decision." Obi said, "I can't lie. I am a little nervous about the whole thing. I have only been working for two years and I am not sure if I want to take on this endeavor at this point of my life." Nkechi said, "Babe, sometimes you have to just seize the moment and let Chineke handle the rest. You have to think about the new possibilities that this will open up for you as well. You have been talking about how you wanted to work with various black community groups. Now you can restructure the firm and do some pro bono work for causes or issues that are important to you." Obi had always just thought about the technical part of the business and totally forgot about the legal aspects that he could explore. He started to become more confident that he could handle the challenge.

After some more time talking, the both of them started to get ready for bed. While the both of them were lying in the bed, Obi and Nkechi were kissing on each other and Obi started to get a little more aggressive to signal he was ready to have sex with her. Nkechi had told him he needed to slow down with everything he was doing. Obi was very frustrated and said to her, "Nkechi, what is the problem. Every time we are close to having sex you always seem not to be interested. Nkechi responded, "That is not the case at all Obi. I know that sex is a very important part of any healthy and functional relationship. But I am not the most sexual person in the world and really have very limited experiences with sex. Also I know you talked about how lively your sex life was with Tamika and I just don't want you to be less interested in me if I can't satisfy you the way she did." Obi said, "Chi Chi, I am not looking for you to be anybody but yourself. You are a great woman and I feel very grateful that I have you in my life as my friend and lover. You already have me interested in you mentally, physically, and emotionally." Nkechi gave Obi a big hug and started kissing on him repeatedly. Obi felt that this would clear the air for them until Nkechi said, "It's that time of the month, so we have to wait a few more days before we can get our freak on." Obi just shook his head and said, "I knew there would be a catch to this at some point. I am happy that you told me about your feelings about having sex with me. I think that us effectively communicating with one another is very important." The rest of the week consisted of Nkechi going to U of H and TSU; checking out their campuses and speaking with advisors in the department she was going to be in. Obi still went to work, but he took some time off and worked from home to hang out with Nkechi as well.

During this time, Obi enjoyed having someone to wake up to in the morning and talk to after he got home from work. He also didn't mind having Nkechi cook breakfast and dinner for him as well. Obi started to think that he could get used to this type of life. As much as he enjoyed being a single bachelor, he knew that it was time for him to have a more stable and less chaotic lifestyle. One day during the week as Obi had come back from work, he saw that his place had been cleaned from top to bottom. He also noticed that Nkechi had placed scented candles around the living room and kitchen area. Obi didn't think too much of it and proceeded to the sofa to watch television. After 15 minutes or so, he saw that Nkechi had come out of his bedroom wearing black clear lingerie, with her breasts and booty popping out. Obi was speechless as he was gazing at her. She came over and shut off the television and put on some R Kelly songs and started giving him a lap dance. Obi was taken aback and excited about what was going on. As she was dancing on him, Obi whispered in her ears jokingly, "I don't have any cash on me, will you stop because of that?"

Nkechi responded, "Don't worry about that, this is your lucky day, I am doing this one on the house." After about ten minutes of dancing, Nkechi and Obi started to have sex with each other. At first there was a little awkwardness between the both of them, but eventually they became comfortable with each other. The sex was pretty good for their first time, except for Nkechi not giving Obi any head because she didn't feel comfortable doing it at the moment. As they were lying on the floor in the living room, Obi said "I can't believe you did the whole strip tease thing." Nkechi laughed and said, "I was really out of my element when I was doing it. But I just wanted to do something spontaneous and special for our first time having sex." Obi said, "Well I thank you for the performance which was fun and thoughtful on your part." Later on that evening the both of them ate dinner and just chilled out. Obi started to see that he was falling in love with Nkechi. Even though he missed the intense and intimate sex that Tamika provided him, he knew Nkechi was really trying her best to make him happy. Nkechi was heading back to D.C. that following Monday.

As Obi was driving Nkechi to the airport, Nkechi's emotions started to get the best of her. "I can't believe how quickly our time together has come and gone. I really had a lot of fun hanging out with you and meeting your family. I just wanted to say that I love you very much and can't wait to be back here in July permanently." Obi said, "Well, I love you too, Chi Chi. It will be interesting to say the least; when we will both live in the same city again." Once they got to the airport, they hugged and gave each other a long intimate goodbye kiss. As Obi was driving back home, he started to think how much he would miss Nkechi's warmth and company. Even though they still had a long way to go, Obi started to think about the whole marriage issue between him and Nkechi. He knew that Nkechi would be clamoring for that once she moved and they were chilling for a couple of months or so after that. As much as he wanted to settle down with her as well, Obi started to think about the talk that he, Lamar, and Chike about how many chances he would have to get any outside pussy. Even though he didn't want to rehash anything again with Tamika, he wouldn't mind having sex with her a few more times before Nkechi would make her return. Tamika was that itch that he couldn't quite get over scratching yet.

The following week the news had reported that Obama would be giving his speech to Muslims in Egypt at the University of Cairo. After that he would be visiting the country of Ghana for a day or so. Obama would not be going to any other African countries on this trip. Obi went to the work the day after the news appeared and his Uncle Ugo was not happy at all. Obi went into Ugo's office to greet him in the morning. "Obi, have you heard this nonsense Obama is doing." Ugo said. Obi responded, "Yes, uncle I found out about it last night.

It is very disappointing news if I might say so myself." Ugo said, "So you are telling me that Clinton and Bush can go to many countries in Africa, but Obama who is African can only go to one. Then he chooses Ghana which borders Nigeria as some type of slap in the face to our country." Obi said, "I read some commentaries on the web from African scholars, like Wole Soyinka, who stated that because of the systemic problems in Nigeria, that the country doesn't deserve to have a presidential visit from Obama."

Ugo started shaking his head in disgust and said, "I have a lot of respect for our academics, but sometimes these guys are too critical of their own people. Is Nigeria the model country of the world? The answer to the question is a resounding no. But are Nigerians along with other Africans that terrible of people that we shouldn't expect to have Obama come visit our countries. No one is telling him to come legitimize some of these rogue governments, but our people are citizens of the world like everyone else. Don't for one minute think that Egypt is any better than anyone else. The leader over there has been in power for over 30 years without any free elections." Obi said, "Yeah, I think it is even worse that he couldn't go to Kenya." Ugo said, "That is a severe miscalculation on his part if you ask me. I heard these guys in his administration say he went in 2006 so he doesn't need to go again. That is a lot of bullshit in my opinion. It is a shame that he can't go to his father's homeland and bring this great honor to his people. This is a huge disgrace for the whole continent of Africa. Obama can go all over the world claiming his Muslim ties, but shrieks about his deeply rooted connection to Africa." Obi decided to change the subject, "Well Uncle I wanted to talk with you about the issues revolving around the law firm." Ugo responded, "So what is it that you to tell me."

Obi said, "I have been thinking a lot the last few weeks and I have come to the conclusion that I would like to take over the law firm." Ugo looked surprised and responded, "Are you sure that this is something that you want to do?" Obi said, "Yes sir, I feel that this will be the best place for me to make the differences that I want to do." Ugo smiled and said, "My nephew, I am very happy that you have come to this decision. It will be a tough challenge, but I will be around to help with anything that you need." Both men embraced each other and then Obi went back to his office. This was one of the biggest moves he had made for his short and long term future.

The next month for Obi was pretty hum drum; he went to work and was talking with Nkechi about their plans for when she would be moving down there. But then in early June, while Obi was his apartment, he received a call from Chike that Ugo had suffered a heart attack. Obi was startled of the news and rushed to the hospital where Chike said he was at. Once he got there, Obi saw that Chike, Aunt Nkiru, and his mother, father, along with Okey and Chinwe were in the waiting room. Everybody was in a very somber mood and just hoping to see what news the doctor would give them. Obi talked with everyone and then he and Chike decided to go outside of the hospital. "So how are you holding up man?" Obi said. Chike responded, "I am doing alright man, just trying to be strong for mama until Chidi and Ngozi come. But to be honest with you cousin I am scared as hell. When I saw him collapse at home, I thought he was going to die before we could make it to the hospital." Obi said, "I can imagine that was a very hard thing to experience. We will put our trust in Chineke to help him recover from this incident." Chike said, "Yes, we will have to just see how things will happen with him.

After about 20 minutes of talking, the both of them headed back into the hospital. As they were walking up, the doctor had just come by and finished talking with the rest of the family. Chike asked his mother what the doctor said. She said, "He will make it, but he can't talk and he has no movement on the left side of his body." Everyone was happy that he wasn't going to die. Obi looked at his father and could tell he was very shaken by everything. He went over to him and said, "Papa, how are you holding up?" Chukwuemeka tried to be stoic and said, "I am doing alright my son; I am just very startled by all of this. I can't believe that we were close to losing Ugo." Chukwuemeka started thinking back to how he came to America for college a few years after Ugo had arrived. He remembers how Ugo was still in law school and working full time as well and how he was able to help him get a partial scholarship to attend Howard University. Ugo never complained about doing it because he was the oldest son of his father and that was a responsibility he had to do for his younger brother.

Chukwuemeka never forgot what Ugo and later on his wife, Nkiru, did for him in his early years in America. Even after he got his engineering degree and went back to Nigeria to work for Shell; Chukwuemeka would always send money and gifts to Ugo's kids on their birthdays and during Christmas time. After about another half hour, the doctor said that it would be fine for Ugo to have visitors. Even though he was not coherent, everyone went in one by one to see Ugo. Obi was the final person to see Ugo for the evening. He broke down and cried on seeing the sight of his uncle. It was hard to see him in such a weakened position. He didn't stay more than a few minutes before he left Ugo's room. As he was driving back home, he began to wrap his self around the notion of death. Even though he didn't think about it too much, Obi knew that his parents were getting older and that their time on this earth was growing lesser by the day. He also couldn't imagine his Uncle Ugo or Aunt Nkiru not being around anymore as well.

Obi also had to come to grips with the fact that starting on Monday he would be running the law firm. He always thought that it would be a smooth transition for him, but with Ugo's heart attack it didn't give anyone enough time to plan everything out. Obi became a little nervous about the whole thing and decided that he needed to take the edge off of the situation. He decided to call Tamika and set up one last round of fucking before it would be truly the end of that part of their relationship. As he was about to give her a call, he received a text message from Nkechi. She just wanted to tell him that she loved him very much and how much she missed him. Obi's conscious got the best of him and he decided he wouldn't do anything with Tamika that night. The next month and a half for Obi was very tough. He was finishing up the cases he had along with the work of his uncle. Obi started to feel trapped by all the new burdens that were now being placed on him. His uncle's medical bills and other debt left almost nothing for Obi to hire another lawyer. It started to seem that on a nightly basis Obi would come home and think about quitting his job. He knew that the private sector wouldn't be easy, but at least he would just be working and not be bothered by other issues. It seemed that the only person keeping him going was Nkechi. She would tell him to hang in there and that once she arrived she would help him out in whatever capacity she could. Obi was relieved when Nkechi had moved down to Houston in the end of July. He was thrilled to have a person who he could come home to and discuss work with in person.

About two weeks after Nkechi had arrived; Obi had received a text message from Tamika. She said that she wanted to meet up with him to talk. He felt that this would be a good time for them to finally discuss ending their sexual relationship. A few days later the two of them met up at a Starbucks. Once Obi saw Tamika he could tell that something looked different with her. Her face had gotten a little more round and she seemed to be a tad bit overweight. Obi asked her, "So is everything okay with you, Tamika?" She hesitated for a minute and then said, "I am doing well, why?" Obi didn't want to draw any attention to the matter and just gave a generic response to her question. Tamika asked him how everything was going on with him at the moment. He told her about everything concerning his uncle and that Nkechi had moved down to Houston for good.

She shook her head and said, "Well it seems like a lot is going on in your life right now. The reason that I wanted to meet up with you is to tell you that I am pregnant." Obi had a stone look on his face after she told him the news. He couldn't fix his mouth to say anything for almost 30 seconds. Before he could utter out a word, Tamika said, "Don't worry you aren't the father. It is this guy that I have been dealing with on and off for the last couple months." Obi let a huge sigh of relief once she told him the second part of the story. Tamika reached over and grabbed Obi's hands and said, "Yeah but I wish you were the father though. I know that you would be there for me every step of the way." Obi was still very subdued on the whole matter but finally blurted out to her, "Congratulations, I know you will do well as a mother." Tamika was a little bit put off by Obi's comment and said, "So is that the only thing you can say to me about this situation. Obi, I am scared as hell about being pregnant and I thought you could have given me a little more moral support." Obi responded, "I am sorry if that is the way it came off to you. But beyond me being a friend for you to talk to, I am unsure what else I can do to help you in this situation." Tamika started to calm down and said, "I guess you are right about that Obi. I guess that I just am on edge right now and just overreacted to your comment." After about another 30 minutes, the both of them left Starbucks and went their separate ways.

While in his car heading back home, Obi couldn't do anything but think about the whole situation. Even though he used condoms with Tamika, he could only imagine the type of situation he would be in at the moment if he was the father of Tamika's baby. There would have been no way he could have explained that situation to Nkechi and his family. But this whole ordeal made him realize how his lustfulness had gotten out of control. He had seen himself incorporate the same practices that Lamar was doing. Once he got home and entered his place, he saw that Nkechi had already had made dinner before she had left to go to one of her night classes at U of H.

As he was eating and watching TV, Obi realized that God had brought Nkechi as a blessing into his life and he had to treat her with the proper care and respect that was due to her. The situations that plagued him at the law firm were still a burden to Obi. Even though Nkechi was here with him for emotional support, the continuous long working hours were still wearing thin on Obi. His uncle's health was improving, but he wasn't at full strength to come back to the office to add any significant help to the staff. Obi began to realize that he wouldn't be able to keep up the pace he was on and began to contemplate reducing the firm's case load and possibly letting go of one of the paralegals. Over the next three weeks, Obi was speaking with his uncle and asking him for advice about what direction he should be heading in regards to the law firm. Ugo didn't really give him any definite answers, he just told Obi that he should do what he thought was best at the time. One day as he came back from work, Nkechi asked him that she wanted to talk with him. As he was settling on the couch drinking a Heineken, the both of them started to have a conversation.

Nkechi said, "Obi, I wanted to talk with you about the law firm." Obi responded, "So in what regards do you want to discuss the matter?" Nkechi said, "I see that running the firm by yourself has been tough on you. I wanted to let you know that I want to help with doing some of the case work until you can find another lawyer." Obi said, "I appreciate you wanting to help honey. But I don't want to take away from your school work." Nkechi responded, "Well don't worry about that, I can work it around my schedule. I also can't sit back and see my man struggle and not do anything about it when I know I can help him out. Nevertheless I probably will be sitting for the bar for this state so working will help me get acquainted with some of the laws out here as well." Obi gave her and big hug and kiss on the lips and said, "Thank you so much Chi Chi. I don't know what I would do without you in my life right now."

Later on that night as the two of them were lying in the bed, Obi started thinking about proposing to Nkechi. Obi knew that he could trust her to always be in his corner through the good and bad times. The next day Obi called Nnamdi to let him know about his decision. "So how is everything going with you and Chi Chi, man?" Nnamdi said. Obi responded, "Everything is going great Zik, I can't complain about nothing. That is part of the reason that I am calling you. I decided that I am going to propose to Nkechi in the next couple of months." Nnamdi said, "Dang man, you ain't wasting any time in moving things since she has moved out there." Obi laughed and said, "You are funny man. But on the real though, I always knew that their something was special about her, but I really didn't get to see it until we started living together." Nnamdi said, "Well you know how I feel about the both of you guys. So I will give you my congratulations in advance."

Obi questioned Nnamdi, "So how are things going with you and Ogechi?" Nnamdi responded, "You know she is starting to get that itch to get more serious and for us to move in together." Obi asked, " So is that something that you want to do right now?" Nnamdi said, "If she had presented this to me earlier this year, I would have flat out shot it down. But I just turned 33 a couple months ago and I started to realize that I have to give up some of my space to let Ogechi get closer to me." Obi responded, "I think that you are making the right decision Zik. Ogechi is a good woman and you have to hold on to her. So it might be back to back weddings for the both of us." Nnamdi laughed and said, "Let us not get too far ahead of ourselves. We will only be getting ready for you and Chi Chi's wedding for right now." Obi agreed and then they talked a little while longer and then ended their conversation.

Obi started to think about how much he would spend on Nkechi's engagement ring and the actual date he would actually propose to her. Obi finally decided he would do it during the first week of October which was around the time of Nkechi's birthday. Obi let his family know of his intentions and he also called her parents to ask them for their blessing in asking for their daughter's hand in marriage. The final step for Obi was to actually pick out the ring. As he began to visit different jewelers, he started to feel the weight of this huge life decision he was about to make come into full view. But regardless of some of his anxiety, he knew that Nkechi was the woman he wanted to spend the rest of his life with. Finally after weeks of getting prepared, the day had come for Obi to propose to Nkechi. Obi had planned to take Nkechi out to dinner to celebrate her 31st birthday and then he would present the ring to her when they got back home. As they were driving back from the restaurant, Nkechi could sense the anticipation on Obi's face. Nkechi said, "So what are you so excited about?" Obi responded, "Nothing I am just happy to be hanging out with you for your birthday." Nkechi smiled and said, "I have a feeling that you are up to something, I just don't know what it is yet."

Once they arrived back home, Nkechi went to the living room to sit down and Obi went into the bedroom to get the ring. " I am about to bring out your present, but you will have to close your eyes first." Obi said. Nkechi laughed and said, "I will play this silly game with you." Once Obi got back to the room he told Nkechi to open her eyes. Obi was on bended knees right in front of her with the ring in the box. Obi said, "Nkechi, I love you so much that words can't explain it right now. You are one of the best things that have ever happened to me in my life. I know that I can't promise you a certain lifestyle of living in a particular neighborhood or driving some luxury cars, but I do know that I will promise to be emotionally, spiritually, and physically with you for the rest of my life. I hope that you can do me the honor of being my wife." Nkechi had tears all over her face after listening to Obi's heartfelt words. Nkechi said, "Obi you know that the answer is yes. I am happy that God was able to put us back together at this point in our lives. I couldn't imagine my life without you being in it." They gave themselves a big hug and kissed each other repeatedly for about five minutes. After Obi and Nkechi called one another's family and friends to tell them the great news, they had sex and went to sleep. A couple of weeks later, Obi celebrated his 30th birthday. Both he and Nkechi found out that she was pregnant and that they would be parents soon.

As he began to digest everything, Obi also began to realize that he now was a grown ass man. But Obi also saw that some dreams he had maybe would have to be postponed. In the near distant future he would be married with a child and the both of them would become his main priority. It seemed with all new things that Obi had going on in his life; he forgot that it had been a year since Obama had won the election. It seemed that the excitement and jubilation from that time about new possibilities had been tampered by the hopelessness and despair of the recession getting more pervasive in the country.

Even though Obama along with Congress had a lot of legislative successes, people began to see that the inspirational man that had galvanized the country to vote for him was now just your standard run of the mill president. It had seemed that Obama was more worried about being liked by Republicans and cutting deals with drug and insurance companies in regards to health care reform than actually framing health care as a moral right every citizen should have access to. But even sadder was the way Obama dealt with black Americans. Even as the recession was brutal, in the black community the unemployment numbers were almost double that of the national average. It seemed that every time Obama was posed with answering that question directly, he would squirm away from it as fast as he could and just say that he was the president of all Americans. Obama also rarely spoke with black representatives in Congress about the issues in their community. If you looked on the surface Obama's support within the black community was still high, but on the outside people started to feel that he was taking them and their issues for granted.

Obama also escalated the amount of troops in Afghanistan as the war over there seemed liked it had no end or direction in sight. As Obi was wrestling about all of these thoughts, he began to reflect on his 30 years of life and the people and experiences he had come across. He thought of a quote from the words of the great William Shakespeare, "All the world is a stage, and all the men and women are merely players, they have their exits and entrances."

ABOUT THE AUTHOR

Chinedu W. Achebe is a Nigerian of Igbo descent who was born in Richmond, Virginia in 1981. He received his undergraduate degree in Economics from the University of Houston and currently resides in Houston, Texas. He is also the oldest of three siblings from Dr. & Mrs. Chukwuma W. Achebe.